Banjo Pickin' Karate Kickin' Crime Fightin' Grandmas

Mike Knudson

D1546549

Books by
Mike Knudson

Raymond & Graham Series

Raymond and Graham: Cool Campers

Raymond and Graham: Bases Loaded

Raymond and Graham: Dancing Dudes

Raymond and Graham Rule the School

Banjo Pickin' Karate Kickin' Crime Fightin' Grandmas

Written by
Mike Knudson

Illustrated by
Vaughan Duck

Silver Lake Press

First published by Silver Lake Press in 2023

ISBN: 979-8-9889099-0-3 (paperback)
ISBN 979-8-9889099-1-0 (ebook)

Illustrations and book design by Vaughan Duck
www.vaughanduck.com

Dedication

For Annette
a true superhero grandma!

Cast of
Characters

Scarlett

Hazel

Izzy

and their Superhero personas

and Supporting Cast

Jackson

Ben

Mrs. Peterson

Ms. Flores

Officer Bagley

Banjo

Award-winning accordionist, Arthur Hernandez, A.K.A. Gramps

Grandma

Izzy's Family

Jack

Max

prologue

Sometimes amazing things happen to ordinary people. Hazel, Scarlett, and I are ordinary girls. I'm not too tall, not too short. I do my homework and don't cause trouble. You probably know a girl like me. Maybe she sits next to you in class, minding her own business, always prepared.

My friend Hazel is loud, dramatic, and excitable, which is why I like her. She's everything that I'm not but sometimes wish

I could be. You probably know someone like her, too.

And every class has the pretty girl. That's Scarlett. Not that Hazel and I are anything too awful to look at, but Scarlett has always been pretty. She never went through that awkward time in life when you're six or seven and you lose your front tooth and a huge new one grows in its place and looks weird because you have one massive tooth next to all your baby teeth. I was in that stage forever—so was Hazel. Scarlett never was.

Anyway, like I said, sometimes amazing things happen to ordinary people. And for Hazel, Scarlett, and me, it happened on Monday, the third week of school, in the lunchroom. I don't want to spoil the story but let me just say we never imagined mystery meat and applesauce would change our lives forever.

Chapter 1

There is Something Strange About Those Lunch Ladies

Hazel dragged her feet along the sidewalk.

"I'm so tired! I can't believe we have to walk to school from now on. These legs were not meant for walking!" she groaned.

"Seriously? We are two blocks from school," Scarlett said. "Plus, walking is good for you. It works different muscles than—"

"Yeah, yeah, I'm sure it does something healthy for me, but it's so slow and tiring!"

We had ridden our bikes to school every

day so far this year. Unfortunately, last Friday my bike was stolen from the school bike rack. I couldn't believe it. It wasn't even that great of a bike.

"You and Scarlett can still ride," I said. "It's not your fault I don't have a bike anymore."

Scarlett let out a huge huff. "Why would you even say that, Izzy? You know we wouldn't make you walk alone—would we, Hazel?"

"Nope, all for one and one for all, even if walking kills me."

I love having friends like Scarlett and Hazel. Even though we're best friends, we are opposites in a lot of ways. Scarlett is way into being healthy. Hazel, not so much. Scarlett likes to keep her long blonde hair perfectly combed, and she is always dressed in the latest styles. Hazel, not so much. Her red curly hair is sort of all over the place, and she doesn't seem to care if what she wears matches or not. As for me, I'm just an ordinary girl. I don't dress in the latest styles, but that's mostly because: one, I'm not really sure what the latest fashions are; and two, I really love sports. I'm even better at sports than most of the boys our age, so I will always choose shoes I can play soccer in at recess before ever choosing to wear uncomfortable fashionable shoes.

"So, what did you guys write your career report on?" I asked. "I wrote mine on being a sports doctor—you know, like a doctor for a professional soccer team."

"I did mine on being a fashion designer," Scarlett said. "I even included some drawings."

Hazel stopped in her tracks. "Wait, those reports are due today? I thought it was next week. I remember Ms. Flores clearly saying they were due next Monday."

"Today is Monday, Hazel," Scarlett said.

Hazel threw her short arms into the air. "But it's not **NEXT** Monday. Today is just regular Monday. I can't believe this! I can't be unprepared again!" She closed her eyes tightly and scrunched up her round face as she tried to squeeze a plan out of her brain. "Okay, how about this... I had to go to the bathroom this morning and, while I was in there, my little brother took my report, made a paper airplane out of it, and threw it out the window." Hazel squinted her eyes up at the sky as though she was watching an invisible airplane. And let's see, then the, um, wind—yes, the wind—

carried it away. And after that, maybe I ran out the door chasing it but—"

"Wait! Stop right there," Scarlett said. "This is so wrong. First of all, why don't you just own it and admit to Ms. Flores that you are unprepared? She must be used to it by now. And second, that is your worst story ever."

I disagreed. "No, the worst story was the time you said you had to draw a map of the neighborhood to help the new mailman find his way around, and the only paper you had was your homework assignment, so you had to choose between turning in your homework and saving the neighborhood from not getting their mail."

Hazel's face lit up. "What do you mean, Izzy? That was a great story! I was a hero. I literally saved the neighborhood!" she said proudly, as if it had actually happened. "Anyway, what's so bad about my airplane story? I think it might work."

Scarlett pulled her long hair over her shoulder. "Really, do I even have to explain?"

"Yes! How else am I supposed to improve my excuses?"

"You could start by just doing your homework."

Hazel ignored that comment and waited for an answer.

"Fine," Scarlett said. "First of all, why do you have to add so many details, especially mentioning you were in the bathroom? Who wants to hear that?"

"I agree," I said. "You are a little too free with gross details."

"But—" Hazel started.

"Second. Your brother is three years old. I've seen how he scribbles in a coloring book. There is no possible way he could fold a piece of paper into an airplane."

"And third—"

"Wait, what if I say my little brother ate my homework instead?"

Scarlett rolled her eyes. "You're kidding, right? You think Ms. Flores would believe your brother *ate* an entire report?"

"But I've already used all the dog excuses: my dog ate my homework, my dog buried my homework, my dog slobbered all over my homework—and then there is the problem that Jackson told Ms. Flores that we don't even have a dog, so I can't use my nonexistent dog anymore in my excuses. You know, if I got a dog for my birthday, it would really come in handy in times like these. I wonder if you can train a dog to eat paper."

Scarlett and I continued walking, leaving Hazel to discuss with herself how she could get her brother to start eating homework.

"Or I wonder if I could train my little brother to eat paper," Hazel continued. "That would be easier since I already have a little brother. Plus, it's about time he steps up and helps his sister out once in a while. Is it too much to ask him to eat *one* assignment now and then?"

After a while she gave up, jogging to catch up with us. "Okay, I'll just tell her the truth."

We made it to our classroom just before the bell rang. Scarlett's desk is in the front row in the corner. Hazel and I sit next to each other in the middle of the classroom. Ben sits behind Hazel. He had his feet resting on her chair.

"Hey, do you mind?" Hazel said, pushing Ben's feet to the floor. Ben loves to bug Hazel every chance he gets. He's been doing it since kindergarten. I think he does it just to get on her nerves. He's like your little brother who sits next to you in the car on a family trip and pokes you for no reason. You tell him to stop, and he does it more. You tell your parents, and he still does it more. You poke him back, and he does it more. You get the picture. That's been Hazel and Ben for the past five years. It's like they have been sitting in the backseat together on a family vacation since kindergarten.

Ms. Flores stood up from her desk in front of the class. "Good morning. I hope you each had a wonderful weekend. And I hope everyone is ready for our career week. I'm excited to learn about the different careers you have researched. We will start this afternoon right after math."

Ben leaned forward. "What's your report on—how to be annoying for a job?" he said to Hazel, laughing at how funny he thought he was.

Hazel turned around, holding up her clenched fist. "No, it's on punching annoying people like you for a job."

Ms. Flores paused. "Hazel, Ben, is there a problem?" That was a daily question from

Ms. Flores. I wondered why she never moved Ben and Hazel away from each other. Ms. Flores is new to our school this year, but she's a great teacher. She's young and funny. She makes subjects fun and exciting.

The morning started normally, like any other day. First, we had a pre-spelling test to introduce the new words for the week. Ms. Flores always gave us a pretest, so we'd know which words to prioritize studying.

She'd tell us the word, then ask someone to use it in a sentence.

"The first word is *quarrel*. Who would like to use it in a sentence?"

Ben's hand shot up. "*Quarrel*. Why does Hazel quarrel so much?" The class laughed.

Hazel raised her hand. "Ben started it today. He told me that—"

"It's just a sentence, Hazel," Ms. Flores said. "Write down the word." She gave us a few seconds to finish writing the word before continuing.

"The second word is *beautiful*."

Scarlett raised her hand. "*Beautiful*. Ben enjoys talking to Hazel because he thinks she is beautiful." (Scarlett can be a little sassy. Plus, she always has Hazel's back.)

Ben's face turned bright red. "What? No, I don't!"

"Write down the word, Ben," Ms. Flores said with a smile. "It's just a sentence."

Since our class was getting a little out of control, Ms. Flores came up with the rest of the sentences on her own.

I won't go into much detail about what happened the rest of the morning, like social studies and science, because I want to get to the really good part. So let me just say that after our spelling test and some other stuff, we lined up by the door for lunch—the lunch that would change our lives forever.

Yep, you heard that right: *Our lives would change forever!*

We were at the front of the line. Hazel always liked to be first, especially in the lunch line. She loved lunch and food of all kinds. Ben pushed his way in front of her.

"I don't think so, Ben. No cutting in line."

"I was here first," Ben said, laughing.

Hazel and Ben struggled for the front spot.

"Hazel, would you please move to the back," Ms. Flores said.

"But I was here first! What about Ben, he just cut in line and—"

"To the back, please."

Hazel hung her head and took her place at the end of the line. Scarlett and I got out of line and joined her. We didn't really care where we were in line.

We were the last class to go through the lunch line. Scarlett asked the lunch lady if she could have extra salad instead of a cookie.

"What? You aren't taking one?" Hazel asked in disbelief, pointing to the large sheet of neatly stacked cookies.

Scarlett didn't answer. After all, it was a ridiculous question. Scarlett only ate "healthy" food. Maybe that's why she was also so tall.

"Come on, Scarlett, you don't *have* to eat it," Hazel begged. "Just put it on your tray, and I'll take it when we get to the table. Plus, we're at the end of the line. They'll have to throw the extras away. Wouldn't that be sad and so wasteful? I know how you feel about wasting stuff."

"You don't want an extra cookie, trust me."

"But I *do* want one!"

"No, you just *think* you want one. You'll thank me later, I promise."

"No, I won't. I would never thank you for keeping me from a cookie. **Please! Please, please, please!**"

"Seriously? You're actually going to beg for a cookie?"

"Please, Scarlett, please." Each time, Hazel begged louder, longer and more annoyingly.

"Scarlett, just get a cookie or we'll never get out of this line," I said.

"Fine! I'll take a cookie."

The old lunch lady picked up a cookie with that clear plastic glove and dropped it onto Scarlett's tray. Scarlett picked it up and stuffed it into Hazel's mouth. "Are you happy?"

"Thank you," Hazel said through her cookie-filled mouth.

Scarlett turned to me. "I still can't believe someone stole your bike right out of the school bike rack. That is just wrong."

"I know. And there is no way I'm getting another one anytime soon. Maybe for Christmas, if I'm lucky, but that's still almost three months away."

"I wish we could find out who did it," Hazel said, spewing cookie crumbs. "I'd really let 'em have it." She punched her fist into her open palm.

"Yeah, me too," Scarlett said. "They'd be sorry."

17

I agreed. "Who gets up in the morning and decides: *Today is the day I am going to steal a little kid's bike*? It's just plain heartless."

"Hey, maybe we can be superheroes when we grow up and catch bad guys," Scarlett joked. "*That* could be our career." She put her fists on her hips and stood tall like a superhero.

"Yes! Scarlett, Izzy, and Hazel save the world!" Hazel added. She stretched her hand out in front of us. "All for one and one for all!"

Scarlett slapped her hand on top of Hazel's. "Yeah. Girl power!"

I followed and we all cheered:

"Girl power!"

We laughed as we continued through the lunch line.

Okay, quick side note for all of you reading this: If you haven't been paying attention so far, this is a good time to start. Because this is where it gets strange.

At that moment, the tall, thin, old lunch

lady leaned over the counter and stuck her wrinkly face in mine. She got so close I could see two long, old lady whiskers sticking out of her chin. An uncontrollable gasp escaped my mouth. Scarlett, Hazel, and I each took a giant step back.

In a raspy, crackly voice, the lunch lady said, "Would you three *really* like to do something about it? You know, *get the bad guys*?" She moved her eyebrows up and down, and the corners of her mouth wrinkled upward.

The second lunch lady—shorter, and equally old—pulled her away by the arm. "Ruby! What do you think you're doing?"

"Come on, Francine, it's time!" the tall one—Ruby—snapped.

By now, a third old lady, who I knew by sight as the one who always seemed to be in charge, waddled over to investigate the commotion. She looked at her two co-workers and then at us. Her thick glasses made her eyes look

enormous. "What is going on over here?"

"Ruby is trying to give these girls... well, let's just say Ruby was about to share our little secret with these nice young ladies."

Scarlett grasped my arm and squeezed.

The boss lady looked at us again and then whispered to Ruby (although her whisper wasn't very quiet). "Are you sure about this?"

Ruby didn't even try to keep her voice down. "Of course I'm sure! We should have passed the power on years ago! It's time!"

The other two threw their hands over Ruby's mouth. "*Shhh!*"

"But why them? They are just little girls." the boss said.

"Why *not* them?" Ruby said. "It's perfect. There are three, and they already said they want to catch bad guys. What more do we need?"

Scarlett's grip on my arm was now painful. We picked up our trays and hurried to a table.

"Okay, that was weird," Scarlett said, opening her carton of milk. "Passed the power on? What do you think they were talking about?"

"I have no idea." I glanced over at the old ladies, who were still huddled, talking. "All I can say is that I'm bringing lunch from home from now on."

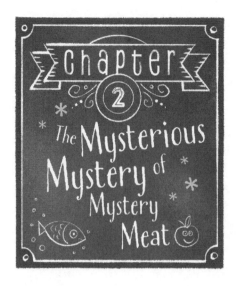

Chapter 2
The Mysterious Mystery of Mystery Meat

Hazel was more interested in her food than the weird old lunch ladies. She pointed to my applesauce. "Hey, are you going to eat that?" Before I could answer, she scooped it onto her tray.

I tried to eat, but every time I looked over to the kitchen, the lunch ladies were watching us. "Are you guys seeing this? Don't look up, but those lunch ladies are still staring at us."

Hazel and Scarlett immediately looked up.

Then those ladies did something they never did—they came out of the kitchen.

Something strange was definitely going on. Those three *never* left the kitchen. In all my years at Spring Valley Elementary, I had never seen those ladies in the halls or anywhere except the lunchroom. When I was in first grade, I thought they lived in there. We froze and stared as they made their way to Ms. Flores. We couldn't hear what they said, but they pointed to us.

"Okay, I am officially freaked out," Scarlett said, standing up. "Let's forget about lunch and go outside." Before we could make our escape, Ms. Flores was at our table.

"Girls, the kitchen staff asked if you three wouldn't mind helping them take inventory in the refrigerator for a few minutes before you go to recess. Would that be okay?"

Scarlett and I looked at each other. I'd never heard of kids counting food for the lunch ladies. I had visions of those women locking us up in the big refrigerator.

"I don't think—" Scarlett began.

"Sure. We'll help," Hazel happily agreed.

I elbowed her in the ribs, and Scarlett gave her the stare of death. It was the same stare she'd given her last summer when Hazel used an entire bottle of Scarlett's pink nail polish to paint polka dots all over her bike.

"What? There is still half a tray of cookies over there," Hazel said, rubbing her ribs.

Scarlett and I ate slowly, trying to avoid our fate for as long as possible. Soon, everyone else had finished, and was out at recess.

Hazel bounced up and down on the bench. "Come on, let's go."

Hazel can be very determined. It can be pretty annoying at times, but mostly it's a good thing. Some of my favorite memories are of things that we did just because Hazel wouldn't drop it until we did it. Like when she begged us to watch scary movies all night at our last sleepover. At first, I tried to talk her out of it. I just wanted to watch something funny and go to sleep. But Hazel always gets her way. By three o'clock in the morning, we had watched three scary movies, and eaten two huge bowls of popcorn and a ton of candy. Every tiny noise in my house caused us to scream. Most of all we laughed like we had never laughed before. That is usually the outcome whenever we finally give in to Hazel.

I quickly scanned the empty tables in the lunchroom. The old ladies monitored us from behind the counter.

"If we die in there," Scarlett mumbled to Hazel, "I'm going to kill you."

We dropped off our lunch trays, and Ruby led us around to the hall door that opens into the kitchen, where the other two ladies stood waiting. The one in charge adjusted her glasses while Francine wrapped a tissue around her finger and began digging in her nose.

"Oh, I am *definitely* bringing lunch from home from now on," I whispered to Scarlett.

Ruby pointed to three folding chairs.

"Please, have a seat, girls. We have some great news. It will just take a moment, and then you can get back to recess."

"Does it involve getting an extra cookie?" Hazel asked. "Or are you going to lock us in the refrigerator like Scarlett and Izzy think?"

"Are you girls comfortable?" Ruby continued, ignoring Hazel. "Because what we're about to tell you is amazing and will change your lives forever." She waved her hands excitedly as she spoke. "In fact, it will be the most—"

"For heaven's sake, Ruby, just spit it out." The boss lady pushed her way in front of the other two. "I'll handle this." She glared at us with those magnified eyeballs. "Look, you three, here's the deal. We're through, done, retired. Got it? No more chasing bad guys, sneaking around late at night—nothing. We're old and tired. It's time for new, younger superheroes to take our place. That's where you three come in."

Francine spoke up. "We've been waiting forever to find the perfect girls to take our places."

"When I heard you three talking about catching bad guys," Ruby added, "I just knew it was meant to be. So, what do you say, girls?"

"Yay, superheroes!" Hazel shouted, jumping up from her chair.

Scarlett grabbed Hazel's arm and pulled her back down.

"What? You don't want to be superheroes?" Hazel asked.

"Superheroes don't exist," I said, standing up. "These ladies are just kidding, or maybe they're just a little... confused." I tried to be polite without flat out calling them senile. "Come on, let's go."

The boss lady shook her head. "You think we're confused? Watch this." She pulled out an old plastic lunch lady hairnet from her apron

pocket and stretched it over her curly, silver hairdo. Then she reached down and with one hand picked up the enormous metal table in the middle of the kitchen like it was a piece of paper. "You call this confused?"

I dropped back into my chair. The old lady carefully set the table back down.

"And what do you think of *this*?" She picked up the huge silver ladle they used to scoop applesauce and bent it in half with two fingers.

"Oh, great," Francine complained. "Now what are we going to use for the applesauce?"

With no effort at all, her boss bent the ladle back to its proper form.

Hazel clapped. **"Awesome!** Do another one!"

Scarlett raised her hand. "How did you—"

The boss lady forced out a deep, loud breath, like we were wasting her time. "Look, I'll give you the short version. Let's just say that one day Ruby dropped a pan of what you kids like to call 'mystery meat' into the applesauce and—"

"Excuse me, but that was an accident," Ruby interrupted. "And I wouldn't have dropped it if Francine here hadn't bumped into me."

"I didn't bump you. You're lucky I was there to catch you!"

"*Catch* me? You mean *trip* me!"

"Oh, so now I tripped you. Well, if I—"

"Enough, you two!" the boss snapped. "You're turning this short version into a long, annoying version." Francine and Ruby quit arguing, and the boss turned back to us and smiled.

"Okay, where was I?"

Hazel's hand shot up. "You were at the part where Ruby drops the mystery meat into the—"

"*Accidentally* drops," Ruby corrected.

"Oh, yes," the boss lady said. "So, Ruby accidentally drops the meat into the applesauce, and that's when it happened."

Hazel leaned forward, her eyes wide. "When what happened?"

"I'll tell you what happened," Francine said. "The whole thing exploded." She threw her hands in the air. **"Boom! Splatter!** Food everywhere! And—**POOF**—suddenly we have these incredible powers. Somehow, enough of that concoction landed on our hairnets, and now, whenever we put them on, the superpowers return."

"Yeah, we're like superninjas," Ruby said, making a pretend karate chop in the air.

"So, there you have it. We're retiring from the superhero gig and handing our nets over to you three. From now on, we are just regular lunch ladies." They each took a wrinkly old plastic hairnet from their apron pockets and dropped them into our laps.

Mystery meat, applesauce, superpowers— I didn't know what to think. Hazel nervously stretched her finger toward the crumpled hairnet, as if some magical powers might zap her.

Scarlett wasn't having any of it.

"Ooh, I don't think so." She picked up the old hairnet with two fingers, holding it as far away from her as possible. "This definitely does not go with anything I wear." In addition to eating healthy, Scarlett is the fifth-grade fashion expert. She has lots of great clothes, and her long hair is always perfect.

I was still confused. "I'm not sure I understand."

The boss lady shook her head and let out another massive sigh. "What's to understand?

You're officially superheroes. Go save the day, get the bad guys, and all that jazz. We're done. The nets are officially yours. The safety of the world is now in your hands. Enjoy." The three ladies hung their aprons on the back of the door.

"So, what happens now? How do we start?" Hazel asked, excitedly. "How do we start fighting crimes? Where are the bad guys? Will you teach us what to do? And how will we—"

The boss lady shook her head, as if Hazel's questions were annoying her. "Look around, there are bad things happening all around you. Like I said, the hairnets are yours now." Then she motioned to her two friends and said, "Let's go, ladies."

"But—" Hazel started.

"Don't worry," Francine said, heading for the door. "You will do just fine. I promise."

Just before leaving, Ruby turned to us and gave us a wrinkly thumbs up. "Good luck, girls.

Oh, and you may want to wait to put those on until you're somewhere private. The first time might be a little awkward. Bye, now." And with that, they disappeared into the hall.

We sat there silently for a few moments.

"Seriously?" Scarlett finally said. "What was that all about?" She and Hazel turned to me as if I would know. Just because I'm really good at math and stuff, Hazel and Scarlett think I should know everything.

"How am I supposed to know?"

Scarlett lifted the hairnet to her nose. "Ooh gross, this smells awful." She walked across the kitchen holding the hairnet in her outstretched arm, keeping it as far away from her as possible before dropping it into the big gray garbage can. "I wouldn't be caught dead wearing something this disgusting on my head, even if it did give me superpowers."

I tossed my hairnet in as well. "It's going to be difficult, but I'm going to try to forget this whole day ever happened. I can't believe we missed recess for this. I'll bet they just wanted to trick us into putting on these smelly old hairnets."

Scarlett agreed. "Yeah, Ben and Jackson probably put them up to this whole thing. They're usually behind anything gross or stinky."

The year before, Ben had hidden his tuna fish sandwich in Hazel's desk over winter break, and when we got back to school the whole room smelled awful. Ben and Jackson thought it was hilarious.

"You're right," I said. "Ben and Jackson are probably outside that door waiting to see us walk out with these big stinky hairnets on our heads. I mean, come on—superheroes? Those three?"

I tiptoed over to the door and quickly opened it, expecting Ben and Jackson to be there. **"Aha!"** I yelled. I looked all around.

The hall was empty.

"But didn't you see her lift the table?" Hazel asked, still clutching the hat.

"That was just a trick," I said. "I'm sure the table is much lighter than it looks." I grabbed the same table leg that she had and tried to lift it. It was actually *heavier* than it looked. I tried again with both hands. Still nothing. We each took a leg and tried to lift it together. After struggling and groaning, we gave up.

I bent over and looked under the table for any clue to how they had pulled off that trick. "You guys can't possibly believe their story?" I said when I found nothing.

"I believe!" Hazel shouted, holding the hairnet tightly against her chest. "Let's do it!" She stretched out the net and lifted it to her head.

"Wait! Stop!

Remember what the lunch lady said about putting them on somewhere private." I said.

Hazel's face lit up. "So, you believe it too, don't you!"

"I don't know what I believe. But just to be safe, let's wait until after school."

"Good idea." Hazel scrunched up her plastic hairnet and shoved it into her pocket.

Just then, the end-of-recess bell rang.

"I can't believe I'm doing this." I reached into the garbage can and grabbed my net.

Hazel and I turned to Scarlett, who was shaking her head. "I just can't do it. Did you smell those? And do you really think that some old, rotten applesauce and mystery meat will give us superpowers?"

"Of course!" Hazel said, as if it made perfect sense. "Come on, Scarlett, all for one and one for all. Please, please, pl—"

Scarlett held up her hand to stop Hazel's begging. (It kills her.)

"Okay, fine!" She stared into the garbage can, and with a disgusted look on her face, she carefully reached in and pulled out the net with two fingers.

We quickly stuffed them into our pockets and ran to class.

Chapter 3

One... Two... Three...

POOF!

Back in class, I couldn't concentrate. All I could think about was the stinky, mysterious hairnet in my pocket. The image of that lunch lady picking up that table like it was a piece of paper was stuck in my brain. I could tell Hazel was thinking about it, too. She was drawing a picture of a supergirl in her notebook instead of copying down the math problems Ms. Flores was writing on the board.

Ben tapped her on the shoulder with his

pencil.

"What?!" Hazel demanded.

As usual, Ben pretended he didn't know what she meant.

"Knock it off, Ben. This is getting old!"

Ben smirked. "Not for me."

"You know you really should be nicer to me. One day I might save your life, or maybe even save the world."

"Yeah, right. What are you going to save me from? Having to smell you?"

"Hey, I don't smell! You do! You smell like a—"

"Are we bothering you two?" Ms. Flores interrupted.

"Hazel was just explaining how she is going to save the world. You know, protect us from aliens or something."

"I didn't say anything about aliens!" Hazel said. "I meant more like superhero stuff—you know, karate chop bad guys, break through walls. Regular superhero stuff."

The class laughed.

"Hey, it could happen!" Hazel said.

Luckily, Ms. Flores stepped in before Hazel said anything else. "While that is very interesting, Hazel, how about we get back to our math problems?" As soon as Ms. Flores turned to the board, Hazel turned back around to Ben.

"Eyes up front, Hazel." Ms. Flores didn't even have to see Hazel to know what she was doing.

Hazel kept quiet the rest of the afternoon. Luckily, she didn't get called on to give her career day presentation. We only had time for three kids to go. Ava talked about being a veterinarian and brought in pictures of her dog with a big cone over its head. She said she also had two cats, a dog, and a fish tank. Courtney talked about being a principal. Finally, Carlos talked about being an airplane pilot. He passed around four different model airplanes. When the final bell rang, we rushed out the door.

"See you tomorrow, Super Hazel," Ben yelled outside. He and Jackson walked off laughing.

Just this morning, Hazel could barely walk the distance to school. Now, she practically ran the entire way to my house.

We all live within a couple of blocks of each other, but my house is the closest to our school. It was time to find out the truth about those hairnets. Scarlett and Hazel called their parents to ask if they could hang out at my house for the afternoon, which they do almost every afternoon.

First, we went to grab a snack from the kitchen. Mom was at the table on her computer. She works from a "home office," which is basically our kitchen.

"Hi, girls, how was your day?"

"Super," I said.

"Yes, super, as in superhero. Right, Izzy?" Hazel added with a giggle.

Luckily, Hazel always says weird things, so Mom didn't think anything of it. Hazel then turned to my six-year-old brother, who had just walked in.

"Hey, Max, do you ever wonder if there are real superheroes out there?"

He opened the refrigerator and pulled a string cheese from the drawer. "The only real superhero is **Spiderman**. Because if you get bit by a red and blue spider, you either die or you become Spiderman." For a six-year-old, Max always seems to have an answer for everything.

45

"Well, what if I told you that maybe one day you would meet a superhero?" Hazel asked.

I grabbed her arm and pulled her away. "Come on, let's go do our homework."

We hurried upstairs and closed my bedroom door.

"What was all that about, Hazel?" Scarlett asked.

"I just think we should create a little mystery for when we become superheroes and start saving the world. You know, like when people start seeing us in superhero masks, but don't know who we are, but maybe they suspect it's us because they heard us talking about superheroes, and then—"

"Wow, you've really thought this through," Scarlett said. "I hate to disappoint you, but I wouldn't count on these stinky hairnets really doing anything but making you want to wash your hair."

"Well, when we are wearing bright red

tights and sparkly capes, you'll see."

Scarlett sat down at my desk and skimmed through a pile of articles I'd printed for school.

"Oh, those are just my current events," I said.

Every day we have to find a news article for school. Ms. Flores was serious about current events. She would let us get away with a lot of things in class, but if a student forgot to bring a current event, it was grounds for missing recess.

Also, even though she is really young, she has lived in seven different states. She always has lots of interesting things to share with our class. She's a great teacher.

Scarlett picked up one of the articles. "Okay, if by chance this whole superhero thing really works, this is the criminal we're going to catch first. Listen to this:

Feline Felon Strikes Again.

Feline Felon Strikes Again.

First Security Bank is the latest victim of what appears to be the work of a serial bank robber who has earned herself the nickname Feline Felon, because of the leopard print mask she wears. A $10,000 reward will be offered to anyone with information leading to her capture."

Hazel bounced excitedly on the bed, staring at the smelly hairnet in her hand. "Let's put these on!"

The more she bounced, the more I thought that just maybe this could work. We were possibly about to become superheroes. "I don't want us to get our hopes up, but just in case this works, we should have some kind of cool superhero stance," I said. "You know what I mean? Like in movies, the superhero is always standing in some awesome pose with their fist in the air or hands on their hips."

Hazel jumped down from my bed. "Great idea! How does this look?" She made a fist and punched the sky.

Scarlett sniffed her hairnet again. "I've changed my mind. The thought of putting this on my head makes me nauseous."

"Come on, Scarlett. We have to do it together," I said. "Plus, just think of all the clothes you could buy with $10,000. You could buy a bazillion pairs of shoes."

"Yeah, come on, Scarlett!" Hazel insisted. "Please, please, please, please—"

"Okay, stop already!" She looked at the wrinkled-up net in her hand. "Well, that *is* a lot of shoes."

"Okay, on the count of three," I said.

"One... two... three."

Hazel's hairnet was on in a flash, and she was back in her superhero stance. I followed. Scarlett put hers on in front of the mirror on the back of my door, careful not to mess up her hair. She gently adjusted it to one side and then tugged it a little to the other side.

"This look is just hopeless," she sighed. "The least they could do is make these out of a more stylish material. I mean, who wears plastic and elastic on their head?"

"So do you guys feel any different?" I asked.

"I think I feel hungrier?" Hazel said.

"She means, do you feel any different than you usually do?" Scarlett asked.

"No, I guess I just feel my normal hungrier self."

I wrapped my arms around my dresser and tried with all my strength to pick it up. Nothing. Even though I knew it was a long shot and probably wouldn't work, down deep I wanted it to be real. For once I thought it would be nice to be more than just the smart girl who is good at sports.

I was about to pull off my hairnet when

Scarlett moaned, "I don't feel so well!"

"Oh my gosh!" I yelled. "Your hair, it's getting—"

"Ouch! My nose!" Hazel screamed. I spun around. Her nose was growing strangely huge.

Suddenly, the weirdness hit me. My nose, my legs, and my arms all felt odd. Finally, we couldn't take it anymore, and we all fell to the ground. As quickly as the weird feeling came, it was gone, and we felt normal again. However, we quickly realized we were far from normal. There was nothing that could have prepared us for what came next. We sat up and looked at each other.

"Aaaah!" we screamed.

To our horror, we had not transformed into superheroes at all, but instead, my ten-year-old friends and I had turned into wrinkly old ladies! We cried hysterically, feeling our wrinkly, saggy faces. At once, we ripped the nets off of our heads and threw them to the floor. Again, a weird feeling rushed over us, and instantly we were back to normal.

We grabbed our faces, making sure they were really okay.

"That was so freaky!" Hazel cried, trying to catch her breath. "You should have seen yourselves. Scarlett, you were so wrinkly. And Izzy, I can't even describe your hideous oldness."

"And you should have seen your nose, Hazel. **It was gargantuan!**" I shouted.

"I knew those old ladies were up to something," Scarlett said, staring at the pile of smelly hats. "What are those things?"

We all fell onto my bed and stared at the

ceiling.

"I don't think I will ever recover from this," Scarlett said. "Those five seconds have scarred me for life."

"Same here. This has been the worst day ever," I added. "I never want to grow old. I hope that's not what we're going to look like when we're grandmas."

"Do you think your mom would mind making us some cupcakes?" Hazel asked.

"Are you kidding?" Scarlett said. "How can you not be completely freaked out? After what just happened, the only thing you can think about is a cupcake?"

"No, my first thought was that it would be nice if we had some chocolate milk. You know, just to help us through this freakiness. But then I thought, *what's better than chocolate milk*? And immediately, chocolate cupcakes came to mind."

"Well, I for one don't think that a cupcake is

going to make this go away," Scarlett said. "In fact, I don't think anything can make—"

"Wait a minute," I said, sitting up. "Do you think—"

"Do we think what?" Scarlett interrupted. "That this was the most disgusting, weird, awful—"

Hazel put her hand over Scarlett's mouth so I could continue.

"Do you think we were superheroes for those five seconds?"

"Who cares?" Scarlett said, pulling Hazel's hand from her mouth. "Who wants to be a superhero if you have to be old and wear a stinky hat? I didn't see any awesome capes or sparkly tights, just old grandmas with bad hairdos. Plus, can you smell that?" Scarlett sniffed the air. "Old people smell!"

"Yeah, I agree with all of that. But what if we weren't just weird old ladies? What if we were actually weird old ladies *with superpowers*?"

I slid off my bed and picked up my hairnet from the floor. "I can't believe I'm saying this, but what if we put these on one more time, just to see? I know it was freaky, but what if we really did have superpowers? Maybe we can get my bike back! Or maybe we really can help catch other bad guys."

"Or even save the world!" Hazel said, picking up her hat. "Let's do it!"

Scarlett shook her head. "No way! Didn't you see us? Not only were we old, but we were so... **UNFASHIONABLE!** I mean what kind of hairdo would you call that mess Izzy was wearing on her head?"

"Come on, Scarlett. We're in this together," Hazel pleaded. "Plus, we can always take them back off!"

We begged and begged until she finally gave in and picked up her hairnet. "I cannot believe I'm agreeing to this. Okay, but no one can know about this—I mean *no one*! I would just die if someone knew it was me in those clothes."

We stretched the hairnets back onto our heads and braced ourselves for the transformation. Again, the weird feeling ... and **POOF,** we were old. For a few moments, we just stared at each other, taking in the freakiness. Then we looked at ourselves in the mirror.

"Whoa, check out my arms," Hazel said. She held up her arm and poked at the hanging skin. "They're all flabby and saggy!"

"What? I can barely hear you guys," Scarlett said, sticking her pinky in her ear and wiggling it around. "And what am I wearing?" It was a big flowery dress that looked like it was a hundred years old. She had an old grandma purse in her hand. "Oh no, please don't tell me I'm wearing baggy pantyhose. This is awful."

"You think that's bad? Look at my bottom!" I announced. **"It's huge!"** I turned around

and shook my new giant backside in front of them.

"Whoa, that is huge!" Hazel laughed. "But look at me—I'm just big all over! And hey, what's this?" Hazel had a big strap over her shoulder connected to something hanging on her back. She pulled it around to the front of her. **"A banjo?"**

We all burst out laughing. Our faces looked even funnier when we laughed, which made us laugh even more. I laughed so hard that a big set of false teeth fell out of my mouth.

Scarlett cringed. "Ooh, yuck! Put those back!"

"Check it out!" Hazel said. We turned to see Hazel holding up my dresser with one hand.

"Oh my gosh! It works!" I said.

We each scrambled for something to pick up. I grabbed the bed and lifted it up over my head. Scarlett picked up my desk like it was a feather.

Carefully, we set everything back down.

Hazel grabbed her banjo and started picking like she had played for years.

"Stop that! My mom is going to hear."

"What do you mean? Look at me go!" She danced around the room as she played. Scarlett grabbed Hazel's hands, stopping her.

Plink-a-plink-a-plink-a-plink-a-plink

"You don't like that?" Hazel asked. "Who

doesn't like 'Foggy Mountain Breakdown'? It's a classic! Wait, how did I know that?"

"Yeah, since when did you become a banjo expert?" Scarlett asked, still holding Hazel's hands away from the banjo strings.

"I don't know, I guess since I put on the hairnet? Scarlett, what's in your purse? Are there any of those hard butterscotch candies grandmas have in their purses? I love those!"

Scarlett started digging around in the small purse. "No, just some tissues, a makeup mirror, and some lipstick. It says the color is

Laser Lips. That's weird." She took off the lid and as she twisted the bottom to make the lipstick come out, a laser beam shot out. It blazed straight across the room and hit a soccer ball in the corner, popping it. We all jumped.

"Whoa! I'm so sorry, Izzy!"

"No problem, I've got plenty of soccer balls. I'm just glad you didn't try to put that lipstick on!"

"That was awesome!" Hazel said, picking up the popped ball, which was still smoking.

False teeth, Laser Lips, banjos, saggy arms—this was getting weirder and weirder. For a moment no one spoke a word. We just sat there, taking it all in.

Finally, Hazel stood up, "Well, girls—I mean, ladies—I mean, extremely old, wrinkly ladies—are you thinking what I'm thinking?" She stretched out her hand. "All for one—"

We stared at her big wrinkly hand, then

Scarlett looked at me and smiled. We slapped our hands on top of Hazel's.

"And one for all! **Girl power!**" we cheered.

"Old, wrinkly girl power, you mean," Scarlett added.

I cinched up my pantyhose, looked into Scarlett and Hazel's eyes, and in my toughest superhero voice said, "Girls, let's go get some bad guys."

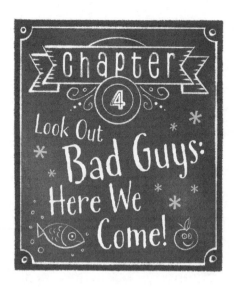

Chapter 4

Look Out Bad Guys: Here We Come!

We took off our hairnets so Mom wouldn't see three old ladies walk down the stairs.

"Hi, Mom. We're just going for a walk around the block."

"A nice walk in this weather sounds wonderful," Mom said. "By the way, what was that music you were listening to upstairs?"

"Oh, that," Hazel said. "That was just 'Foggy Mountain Breakdown' by the famous Earl Scruggs, the best banjo player to ever live.

He really made the three-finger-picking style popular when he developed—"

"Hazel is doing a report on folk music for our class," I interrupted.

Mom smiled. "Wow, that's very impressive, Hazel."

Once outside we looked for a place where we could slip on our hairnets without making a scene.

"How about in the clubhouse?" Hazel suggested. We hurried to the side of the house behind two large pine trees. There was no actual clubhouse, but we used to pretend the little space between the trees was our girls-only club when we were in the second grade. We would hang sheets between the trees and the fence. We stopped hanging up the sheets a long time ago, but it is still our secret place.

We pulled on our hairnets and, instantly, we were wrinkly again.

"Okay, just walk out and act natural," I said.

Hazel nodded. "Natural, got it."

She stepped out from behind the tree and shouted, "Okay, my old lady friends, it, um, looks like this tree is just perfect."

Scarlett followed. "Yes, I agree, my normal, old, wrinkly grandma friend." She was speaking even louder than Hazel. "This tree seems to have just the right number of branches."

I shook my head and followed. "Old women counting tree branches? Yeah, that's normal."

"Normal? Just look at us," Scarlett said. "How normal can we look? Don't you think we stick out walking around the streets wearing these things on our heads?"

"Who cares," Hazel said. "That's the best thing about being old; you can do anything you want. You can wear weird clothes, walk around with these big flabby arms, and say weird things. Old people don't care what they look like. Otherwise, they wouldn't dress like they do."

"Well, I care," Scarlett said. "There's no law that says you can't dress nice just because you're old. And can you guys please speak up a little? I can barely hear you."

"I'm with you," I added. "I'm no fashion expert, but look at our shoes. Why do we have these high-top sneakers when we're wearing dresses? How many grandmas do you see playing basketball?" I pretended to jump up and shoot a basket. However, when I jumped, I flew about twenty feet into the air. **"Wow!** I think I just figured out why we're wearing these sneakers." Not only could I jump incredibly high, but I could also run like lightning. I ran down to the end of the street and back in the blink of an eye.

"Hey, I'm fast, too," Scarlett said, zipping around us in circles.

"Yay! I'm finally fast!" Hazel said, excitedly. But when she tried to run, she wasn't any faster than her ten-year-old self. "Hey, no fair. Where's my speed?"

"Oh, my gosh, I wonder if we can fly!" Scarlett exclaimed.

Hazel's eyes lit up. "Me first, me first!" She put her hands in the air, closed her eyes, and yelled, "To the sky!" She scrunched her face tighter and pushed her fists higher into the air, but it was no use. She opened her eyes only to find herself still standing on the sidewalk. "Hey, maybe if one of you gives me a little boost."

"What do you mean?"

"You know, pick me up and throw me up to the sky. I'm sure my superflying power will kick in."

I looked up and then back at Hazel. "I don't know, it seems kind of dangerous. What if you can't fly and get hurt?"

"I'll be fine. Scarlett can throw me, and if I start to fall, you can run up superfast and catch me." We looked around, making sure the coast was clear. Then Scarlett lifted Hazel up over her head.

"Ready?"

Hazel gave her a thumbs up. **"Fire away!"** Without any effort at all, Scarlett sent Hazel soaring into the sky.

"It works! I'm flying!" she shouted with joy, rocketing higher and higher.

"Wow! She's really doing it!"

"It's sort of beautiful, isn't it, Hazel up there flying like a bird?" I said, watching our friend soar through the sky. Her dress, saggy arms, and chubby cheeks were flapping all over the place.

Scarlett shook her head. "No, I don't think beautiful is the word for that."

A moment later, Hazel slowed down and began to fall. **"Help!"** she screamed, plummeting toward the ground.

She was coming down about six houses

away. I raced over as fast as I could. Two little kids were riding their bikes on the driveway.

Hazel was falling fast, screaming the whole way. I held out my arms and moved side to side, trying to calculate her landing spot. At the last moment, I closed my eyes and held my breath. It felt like being hit by a gigantic marshmallow. The force knocked me backward. Luckily, my huge bottom softened my fall. The kids dropped their bikes and ran into the house screaming.

Scarlett raced up to us. "We'd better get out of here. Hop on, Hazel. I'll give you a piggyback ride."

"So, I can't run, jump, or fly?" Hazel muttered as we ran. "I guess I'm just a strong, overweight, old lady."

"No; you're a strong, overweight, old lady that can play the banjo," Scarlett corrected.

"Don't worry," I said. "With our speed and strength, we can still catch bad guys and do all kinds of stuff. The only problem is figuring out how to find these bad guys?"

Scarlett let Hazel down a couple of blocks away, and we walked around searching for any signs of evildoers in the act of sinister activity, but it was apparently a slow day for criminals. The only person we saw was a lady walking a dog.

"Hmm, do you think that lady stole that dog?" Hazel whispered.

"I think she's just walking her dog," I said.

"That's just what a dog stealer would want you to think. There's only one way to find out."

Before we could stop her, Hazel walked up to the lady. "Hello, we are patrolling the neighborhood and want to make sure this is actually your dog and that you aren't really a dog thief disguised as a regular citizen."

The lady tugged nervously on the leash, pulling her puppy close to her. She slowly backed away from Hazel.

Hazel intensified her stare. "Your silence makes me wonder if you're hiding something." She pulled her banjo around and played some suspenseful music.

Scarlett and I each grabbed one of Hazel's arms and pulled her away.

"We are sorry, ma'am. Have a nice day," I said.

"Hazel, what is wrong with you?" Scarlett scolded.

"What? How are we ever going to find any criminals if we don't investigate?"

"We can't just walk up to people and ask if they're thieves," I said. "Plus, do you think real criminals would simply tell us that they're criminals?"

We agreed that we needed to be sneakier. We decided to hide and wait for criminals to come to us.

"How about over there?" Hazel said. She pointed to some bushes against a house.

"We could hide behind those."

"Really?" Scarlett said. "Hiding in bushes? If this is what superhero life is all about, I don't think I want to do it anymore."

Hazel was already halfway to the bushes. "Come on, you guys, this will be fun. It's like a stakeout."

"Fine. Five minutes, Hazel. I'm not sitting in bushes for more than five minutes."

"Okay, who brought the binoculars?" Hazel asked, as if we had a bunch of tactical gear with us.

With no response, Hazel made two circles with her hands and held them up to her face as if they were binoculars.

"What are you doing?" Scarlett asked.

"*Shh*, I'm surveying the street."

"Whatever," Scarlett said. She then turned to me. "Izzy, I still don't get the math assignment on fractions. What do you do when—"

"Can you guys keep it down?" Hazel

complained. "You're going to scare away the criminals."

Just then, a car pulled into the driveway. A mother and her two little kids got out. As they walked up to the front door, one of the kids spotted us in the bushes.

The mom gasped and pulled the kids behind her like she was protecting them from wild animals.

I jumped up. "Hello, we're sorry to have startled you by sitting here in your bushes. We

were just, um..." I couldn't think of a good reason for sitting in someone's bushes.

Hazel stood up with her pretend binoculars still up to her face. "We are just patrolling the neighborhood, keeping nice people like you safe."

Scarlett reached over and pulled Hazel's pretend hand-binoculars down from her eyes. "We were just leaving."

Once the lady and her kids were inside, Scarlett picked Hazel up and we all sped away

with our superspeed, stopping a few blocks away.

I was ready to give up on the superhero thing when Scarlett noticed something.

"Hey, there's your bike, Izzy!"

"Where?"

"Right there, on the porch of that house with the green van parked in front."

Hazel and I squinted. We couldn't see anything.

"Are you talking about way down there?" Hazel pointed to a house all the way at the end of the long road. I could barely tell that the car parked in front was a van. And there was no way I could tell what was on the porch.

"Yeah, that one," Scarlett said. "I'd recognize your bike anywhere."

"How can you see that far?" I asked, still squinting.

"No way! You have superhero vision, don't

you?" Hazel cried. She shook her flabby arms in the air. "No fair! I want more superpowers!"

We raced down to see if it was really my bike, and sure enough, it was. It had my same seat, handlebars, and everything.

"What should we do?" I asked.

"What do you mean?" Scarlett said. "We should take it back—after all, it's your bike."

"Yay! Our first crime!" Hazel said. "Though I wish we could fight some bad guys in masks to get your bike back." She punched her fist into her hand. "That would be so awesome!"

Scarlett was getting excited now that we had an actual crime to solve. "Yeah, remember earlier at lunch? We were really going to let 'em have it if we ever found out who stole your bike. I say we get the thief!"

Even with superpowers, I was a little nervous.

"Let me go talk to them. Maybe they just accidentally took it."

Scarlett and Hazel waited by the curb while I walked up and rang the doorbell. A man about my dad's age opened the door. He looked at me from head to toe, or from hairnet to high-top sneaker.

"May I help you, ma'am?"

I looked around to see who he was talking to before realizing it was me. I'd never been called *ma'am* before.

"Yes, I think there may have been a mistake. You see, that's mine." I pointed to my bike. "It was stolen from school Friday. I'm sure it was a mistake, but—"

He looked at my bike and then back at me. "I'm sorry, this isn't your bike."

"Yes, it actually is my bike." We went back and forth a couple of times until he got angry and demanded I get off his property. Nervously, I rushed back to Scarlett and Hazel.

"What?" Hazel yelled. "He told you to get off his property? But that's your stolen property on his property! Come on, ladies, let's get that bike." Again, Hazel punched her fist into her hand.

"Maybe this whole superhero thing isn't really the best approach," I said. "Maybe we should talk to him again."

"You already tried that. The time for talking is over. It's time for action." Hazel sounded like she was in some kind of action movie. She practiced a couple of karate kicks and boxing punches in the air as she walked up the steps to the house. Scarlett and I followed behind. Hazel picked up the bike with one hand, and we started back toward the street. She was halfway down the driveway when the door opened.

"Hey, put that down," the man shouted. "I told you to get off my property."

"I don't think so, Buster!" Hazel yelled. She set the bike down and put up her fists like she was going to fight the man. Then she turned to us. "Izzy, Scarlett, make some fighting poses," she whispered. I put up my fists like Hazel. Scarlett looked confused, like she wasn't sure what to do, so she just waved her arms around and made spooky ghost sounds.

"We're taking the bike back whether you like it or not, bub," Hazel growled.

The man started down the steps toward us, not looking scared at all.

"Okay, you leave us no choice," Hazel warned. "Girls, show Mister Bike Stealer here what we can do. Pick up that big rock over there, Scarlett."

Scarlett looked at the huge dirty boulder and then chose a small cleaner pebble lying on the driveway.

"How about this one? The other looks a little dirty."

The man kept walking. I stepped over and, with one hand, picked up the giant boulder in the garden. Then Hazel leaned over and lifted half of his car up with one hand. With her other hand she made a fist and flexed her saggy arm.

"Are you sure you want a piece of this?" She set the car down and took one step toward the man. "The way I see it, you can apologize and crawl back into your house like the bike-stealing coward you are, or we can start busting heads." The man's face instantly drained of all color, and he slowly backed up, tripping on the porch step. He scrambled to his feet and scurried frantically into his house. We could hear the sound of the door locking.

"Good choice!" Hazel shouted through the door.

We grabbed the bike and started down the road.

"I can't believe it, Hazel," I said. "What came over you? You were so tough and—I don't know—in charge."

Hazel smiled. "I know. It felt great. This superhero thing really feels natural." She raised her hands in front of her face. "It's like I was born for this! Although, what was that wavy thing you were doing with your arms, Scarlett?"

"You told us to make frightening poses. That was the only thing I could come up with."

"*Fighting* poses, not *frightening* poses," Hazel said.

"Ah, that makes more sense," Scarlett said.

"Oh well; at least we solved our first crime. We should celebrate."

"Plus, we're back to riding to school!" I added.

I got on my bike and started pedaling alongside my friends. Immediately, I noticed that something was wrong. "Wait a minute. This doesn't feel right."

"Of course it doesn't," Scarlett said. "Your bottom is like ten times its normal size. You need a bigger seat."

"No, it's not that." I got off and took a closer look at the handlebars. "I think maybe that guy was right. I don't think this is my bike. The grips on my handlebars were squishy, not hard like these." I examined the bike more closely. "And remember the first day we rode to school? I didn't have my lock and so we locked it together with yours."

Hazel nodded. "Yeah, I remember. Both of our bikes got all scratched up in the front."

I pointed to the front of the bike. "Look, no scratches."

Hazel leaned down to take a closer look. She rubbed her hand along the front of the bike where there should have been scratches. "Oh no! What have we done? That guy was no criminal at all."

"Unless you count him wearing socks with his sandals," Scarlett said. "Did you guys see that? Now *that* should be against the law."

I picked up the bike and started back. "Come on; we need to apologize." We put the bike back on the porch and rang the doorbell. No one answered. I imagined he was still scared to death. Hazel opened the mail slot on the front door and shoved her face up to it.

"Hello in there!" she called out. "It's me, Hazel, the old superlady who was going to bust your head."

"Hazel!" I said, pulling her face away from the door and putting mine in its place.

"Excuse me, sir, we've made a terrible mistake. Your bike is back where we found it. We're very sorry. Have a nice day."

"And by the way—just a friendly suggestion," Scarlett said, squeezing her face beside mine. "Socks and sandals never mix. Just letting you know. Bye-bye, now."

"I can't believe we almost stole that bike," I said. "Maybe we're not ready for these powers. We are scaring kids, accusing people of being dog stealers, sitting in people's bushes freaking them out, and now we're bike thieves. We are more troublemakers than superheroes."

"Of course we're ready," Hazel said. "So we made a little mistake. Who cares? We put the bike back. Plus, this superstrength is awesome!" She held her hands up in front of her face like she could feel power racing through them. "We are going to clean this town of every bad guy."

"Well, so far *we're* the only bad guys," I said.

As we got to the street, a police car drove up. We froze in our tracks.

"What do we do? Let's make a run for it!" Hazel suggested.

"Don't be silly," Scarlett said. "We aren't criminals. Just stay calm."

A policeman stepped out and introduced himself as Officer Bagley. Just then, the man from the house ran out.

"That's them, officer. The ladies who stole my daughter's bike."

The officer looked at the man, then at us. He scratched his head. "Are you saying these three old—"

"Hey, who are you calling old?" Hazel interrupted.

"Forgive me, I mean are you telling me that these three *young* ladies stole your bike— that bike on your porch?"

"Yes. And they said they were going to bust my head."

Hazel couldn't help giggling. She put her hand over her mouth to keep her laugh from escaping.

"Then that one picked up this huge boulder, and this one picked up my car and—"

"Hold on, sir. Do you really want me to write a report stating that these ladies picked up boulders and cars?"

Suddenly, the man looked confused. He looked at the car, then at us, and then back at Officer Bagley. "I... um..."

"Are you okay, sir?" the officer asked. The man was silent for a moment before slowly returning to his house, mumbling and shaking his head.

"I'm sorry for the trouble, ladies," the policeman said.

"It's quite alright, Officer Baggy," Scarlett said.

"That's Bagley, ma'am," he answered, "with an 'L'." As we watched him drive away, we decided we'd be much more careful next time before picking up cars and busting heads.

On the way back home, I asked Scarlett

and Hazel why we had never heard of real superheroes before. "If those old lunch ladies have been doing superhero stuff all of these years, why weren't they in the news? Why hasn't anyone ever seen them?"

"Probably because they mastered the art of the ninja," Hazel said.

"Come on, Hazel," Scarlett said. "We have the same powers, and already on our first day, people are calling the police on us. I'm with you, Izzy. Why haven't we ever heard of these superheroes?"

We discussed it all the way home. Once back at my house, we went behind the tree, took off our hats, and sat on the grass.

"It feels good to have my normal face again," I said, rubbing my smooth skin.

Scarlett agreed, running her fingers through her hair.

"I don't know. I kind of miss my flabby arms," Hazel said.

"So, what are we going to do next?" I asked.

Hazel rubbed her stomach. "Well, I don't know about you two, but I'm going home for dinner."

Chapter 5

The Amazing Dodgeball Master

"Mom, I'm home."

"How come it's always '*Mom*, I'm home'?" Dad said, carrying a suitcase down from upstairs. "How about now and then it's, '*Dad*, I'm home.'?"

"Hey, Dad, you're home early." I ran up and gave him a hug. My family is awesome.

"Yep. Mom is coming with me to the convention tomorrow. I took the afternoon off to help pack and get ready. And Max here will be in charge while we are away—right, son?"

"Yes! Can I send Izzy and Jack to their rooms whenever I want?" Max said, too eagerly.

"Of course you can. Just make sure you let them out once in a while to eat." Like most dads, my dad thinks he's hilarious.

My older brother, Jack, walked in with his guitar. He's fourteen and thinks he's a rock star.

"I'm glad you're all here. What you are about to hear is the greatest love song ever written." He sat down on the couch and started strumming. That's the other thing about Jack: He'd turned goo-goo about girls. Every day it's someone else at school that he is totally in love with.

"This came to me in math class today," he said. "It was inspired by my soon-to-be girlfriend, Claire, who sits next to me."

"What does 'soon-to-be' mean?" Dad asked.

"It means that she doesn't know it yet, but

it is meant to be—it's destiny. It will all make sense after you hear the song."

He started strumming and singing about needing Claire like he needs air; then he threw in something about math class and a random line about the planets and the ocean. It made absolutely no sense. When he finished, he hung his head and let out a big sigh, as if the song had drained him of all energy. We stood there wondering what was wrong with him.

Suddenly his head popped back up as if nothing had happened. "Wait, did you say you and Mom are going out of town? Does that mean Grandma and Grandpa are staying over? Can you please tell them I'm on a special diet, and the doctor says I can only eat cereal and sandwiches?"

Dad travels a lot for work and every now and then Mom goes with him. Grandma and Grandpa stay with us when they go. They are great, and we love them. The only downside is dinner. Normally, our family eats regular food for dinner—you know, spaghetti, chicken, tacos, and every now and then if someone doesn't like what we are having, they just grab a bowl of cold cereal or something. But with Grandma and Grandpa, we always have to sit down together and eat whatever Grandma cooks. There is no complaining and no leaving any food on your plate, period. You stay at the table until you are done. Usually, it's okay, but at least one meal during their stay, Grandma cooks something terrible like liver and onions or some weird mushy vegetable that you've never heard of.

Mom walked into the room with her phone pressed against her ear. "Of course, Mother, I just got back from the store and bought everything on your list, except liver—they were out of that... Great, we will see you in the morning... bye-bye."

Mom slid her phone into her pocket.

"I think I saved you from liver and onions this time. How was your afternoon, Izzy?"

In my head I was saying,

Well, I turned into an eighty-year-old supergrandma, I caught Hazel as she fell from the sky, and I stole a bike.

But instead, what came out was, "It was okay."

"Wonderful. Your father and I will only be gone for three days. And Grandma said she will be happy to attend your parent-teacher conference, since we will miss that."

"Can you tell Grandpa to only use the bathroom in the basement, please?" Max said. "He stinks up the whole house!"

"Yes!" Jack agreed. "Nice call, little man. That should always be an official rule for Grandpa."

"Let's be polite, Max," Mom said.

I had to agree with Max and Jack. Maybe it was all of that weird food Grandma cooked.

"And they will also take you to your soccer game, Izzy. Grandpa is excited for that."

"That's okay. The game is just at our school—I can walk." The last time Grandma and Grandpa had come to a game, it was so embarrassing. I love them both, but they talked about weird things with the other parents, and they don't know much about soccer. Last time, Grandpa yelled **"Touchdown!"** when I kicked a goal.

After dinner, I searched online for a current event for the next day. Now that I was sort of a superhero, or kind of becoming one, I looked at the news differently. I read about cars and other things getting stolen, news about executives of companies doing illegal things, and all sorts of other criminal things happening. I wondered if I could ever really make a difference, even as a superhero, especially after the trouble we'd caused that afternoon. I changed into my pajamas, brushed my teeth, and climbed into bed.

Mom came in and sat on my bed to say goodnight.

"Mom, this is a weird question, but do you think superheroes are real? Do you think people can really make the world better?"

"Of course, Izzy. Anyone can be a superhero and make a difference. You make a difference in our family every day. And you are a good friend to others. Yes, superheroes come in all shapes and sizes."

Just then, Max ran down the hall past my doorway in nothing but his Spiderman underpants.

"See," Mom said, laughing.

"There goes one now."

I wanted to tell her I meant real superheroes with superstrength and other superpowers, but I didn't.

"Goodnight, Izzy. I'd better go catch Spiderman and get him to bed."

"Goodnight, Mom. Love you!"

"Love you, too."

I said my prayers and went to bed.

The next morning, I was on the porch early waiting for Hazel and Scarlett to walk to school. Since we couldn't ride bikes anymore, we had to leave much earlier than normal.

As we walked, we relived every moment from our bike-stealing episode the day before.

"I can't wait for lunch today," Hazel said. "I need to talk to those lunch ladies. It's not fair that I don't have superspeed or incredible jumping powers like you two. Maybe we can trade powers. Maybe I can run fast, and Scarlett, you can have my banjo."

"Why would I want your banjo?"

"I don't know, because then you could play all of this random music and have your head filled with useless banjo facts that nobody cares about."

"Well, as fun as that sounds, I think I'll stick with superspeed. But I would like to ask them how we can get different clothes."

"And I'm wondering if my superhero bottom needs to be so huge," I said. "Doesn't it seem like I would be more ninja-like if my backside were a little smaller? I wonder if there is a way to make that happen."

"Hey Izzy, did you get that last word problem on our math assignment about eating half a corn dog and drinking two-thirds of a soda? It didn't make any sense to me at all," Scarlett asked. "Plus, I can't imagine ever eating anything as disgusting as a corn dog. They are made with—"

"Oh, I love corn dogs!" Hazel interrupted. "Have you ever had one at the state fair? They are pure heaven." Hazel's eyes closed as she dreamed of the glorious state fair corn dogs. Then her eyes popped back open. "Oh, no! The math assignment. I got so annoyed with Ben yesterday in class and then spent the rest of the time drawing superheroes. I forgot all about the assignment. This will be the second assignment that I haven't done this week. All right, let me think. What if I say my neighbor's dog ate—"

"Not again," Scarlett said.

"But it wouldn't be *my* dog, it would be my neighbor's."

We ignored her and kept walking.

"Fine. I'll tell the truth. But I hope you guys are happy next year when you're in middle school and I'm still back in fifth grade."

We got to school, and I remembered it was Tuesday, my favorite day. It meant PE first thing in the morning. As usual, Ms. Flores lined us up, and we walked single file to the gym in complete silence. One peep from anyone and she would march us back to class and start over. Hazel was usually the noisy culprit. She had a hard time keeping her mouth shut, even for two minutes.

This time she managed to keep quiet almost the entire way. We were about ten feet from the gym when she couldn't take it any longer. **"Yes! I made it!"** she exclaimed. Our entire class turned and glared. She had done that once before when we were only a few steps away, and we had to start over. Luckily, this time, Ms. Flores ignored Hazel's outburst and led us into the gym, where she left us with Ms. Brown, our gym teacher.

Ms. Brown had us run two laps around the

gymnasium before announcing that we would be playing dodgeball. (I love dodgeball. Scarlett hates it.)

"Why do we have to play dodgeball again? Last time I broke two fingernails. They're just barely growing back. *Look*." She stuck her left hand up to my face. "Seriously, I'm going to pretend to get hit and to get out of the game."

"And if Ben hits me again, I swear I'm going to do something drastic," Hazel added.

"Come on," I said, "it's just a game."

Just as we got all the balls out of the closet and divided into teams, a voice came over the intercom: "Ms. Brown, could you please come to the office."

"Okay class, remember the rules. No throwing hard at close distances and only aim below the shoulders. I'll be back in a few minutes. Courtney will be in charge while I'm gone." I don't know why, but teachers always ask Courtney to take over when they go to the office. Courtney is extremely serious and never has a problem reporting us to the teacher. She is even stricter than Ms. Flores. I don't think I have ever seen her smile except when she is telling on someone.

After setting the balls on the middle line, we took our spots on each side of the gym. Courtney blew the whistle, and we raced to grab a ball. In no time, balls were flying everywhere. Scarlett immediately faked getting hit and sat down on the side. Ben had a ball in his hand and was waiting for the perfect shot at Hazel. She moved around, trying not to be an easy target, but just like always, he wound up and threw the ball as hard as he could. She spun around and **SMACK,** the ball hit her right in the middle of her back. Ben laughed his head off.

Hazel's face turned red and she clenched her fists. I thought she was going to explode. Then, out of nowhere, a smile crept onto her face, and she calmly walked to the door.

"May I use the restroom?" she asked Courtney. "It's kind of an emergency."

Courtney nodded, and Hazel disappeared out the door. She was up to something. Ten seconds later, one of the lunch ladies walked in.

It was superhero Hazel!

"What is she doing?" Scarlett whispered.

"Hello, kids!" Hazel announced. "I'm just waiting for the spaghetti to cook in the kitchen. You youngsters don't mind if I join in the fun while I'm waiting? I was pretty good at dodgeball back in the day. Back then, the ball hadn't been invented yet, so we had to use rocks. It made us tough."

The entire class fell silent. No one knew what to say.

"Well, what are we waiting for? Are we playing or what?" Hazel said.

"You can be on their team," Ben said, pointing to our side.

"Great! Let's play." Even though Hazel danced around, taunting the other team, no one dared throw a ball at an old lady. Finally, it was down to Hazel and me on our side and Ben and Jackson on the other. Ben and Jackson each threw a ball at me at the same time. I dodged Ben's, but Jackson's throw hit me in the foot.

"You're out!" he yelled.

As Jackson celebrated, Hazel hit him with a ball.

"You're out, too, shrimp!" she cackled. Scarlett and I looked at each other and giggled. The rest of the class laughed.

"Looks like it's just you and me, Ben," Hazel said.

"Hey, how do you know my name?"

"Come on, do you want to talk or play?" Hazel replied, dancing around.

Our entire class was now standing and cheering for their teams.

He picked up a ball and threw it at her. She easily dodged it. Even though she didn't have superspeed, she could dart around quickly like a ninja. Ben threw another and another. He still couldn't hit her. Jackson and his friends laughed. Finally, he ran out of balls.

"Looks like you're out of ammo," Hazel said. She picked up a ball in each hand. She rolled one to the back corner of Ben's side of the gym. "Here you go." As he turned and bent over to pick up the ball, Hazel wound her arm back and threw the ball at about a thousand miles per hour, hitting Ben squarely on his bottom, knocking him to the floor.

"Yeeoow!" Ben lay on the ground, rolling around and rubbing his backside. The class exploded with laughter.

"Hooray, we win!" Hazel called out. Then she quickly exited out the door. A few seconds later, ten-year-old Hazel returned. The whole class was still laughing. Even Courtney was enjoying it all.

"What's so funny, Izzy?" Hazel said.

"Well, it seems that a very strong lunch lady came in and decided to play dodgeball with us. She hit Ben pretty hard with the ball. It's probably something she shouldn't have done. Something that could get her in a lot of trouble, if you know what I mean."

"Hey, that wasn't fair," Ben complained, from the floor. "She wasn't really on your team. That gave you an extra player."

"Come on," Scarlett replied. "You're going to complain that it wasn't fair because you got beat by an old granny?"

Jackson held his hand out and pulled Ben to his feet. "Dude, that's just too embarrassing."

Just then, Ms. Brown returned. "It sounds like you've been having fun while I was gone."

"Everyone except Ben," Jackson said.

"What happened? Ben, is everything okay?"

"Yes, everything's fine," Ben grumbled.

I pulled Scarlett and Hazel away from the crowd. "We need to make some rules. That could have gone really bad."

They both nodded.

"I'm sorry," Hazel said, trying not to smile.

I did my best to keep a straight face, but finally gave up and burst out laughing. "Okay, I have to admit that was pretty good."

We went back to class for social studies and reading before lining up again for lunch. Hazel, Scarlett, and I moved to the end of the line so we could talk to the lunch ladies without anyone hearing.

"Okay," Scarlett said. "The first thing we

need to find out is how we can get more stylish old-lady clothes."

Hazel disagreed. "Who cares about that? First, we need to find out what's up with the banjo and how I can get more powers like you guys."

"Wait, don't you think we should find out what kind of crimes we should be solving?" I said. "That seems like the first thing we should ask. We need some superhero instructions."

"You think that's more important than our clothes?" Scarlett asked.

We argued back and forth until Ms. Flores stepped in.

"Girls, is there a problem? We're not going to lunch until we are all quiet."

"Sorry," we answered together.

Hazel leaned over to Scarlett and whispered in her ear,

"Superpowers."

Without moving her lips, Scarlett quietly replied,

"Clothes."

"Superpowers,"

Hazel softly shot back.

"Clothes,"

Scarlett replied almost silently.

They went back and forth quietly like that all the way to the lunchroom. Finally, Hazel gave up. But as Scarlett picked up her lunch tray, I heard a soft whisper say,

"Superpowers."

We took our time picking up our trays and silverware so there would be plenty of space between us and the other students. Finally, the last kids started toward the tables.

"Excuse me," I said. "We really need to talk to you ladies."

Francine leaned forward. "Is something wrong, dear? Would you like more carrots?"

"Yes, something is very wrong," I said. "You see, we put on the hairnets, and—"

"Here's the thing," Hazel interrupted. "Scarlett wants new clothes, Izzy's bottom is huge, and I want to fly or get some other cool powers like them."

"I was thinking maybe a nice skirt and silk

top," Scarlett said. "That awful dress does nothing for me."

"What's the hold-up?" Ruby said from the applesauce tub.

"I don't know. For some reason these young ladies are asking for more than food. For instance," Francine said, pointing, "this one is demanding new clothes, that one wants to fly, and the short one has a big bottom."

Ruby smiled. "Don't worry about your bottom. You're still growing. I'm sure the rest of your body will catch up."

"I'm not talking about right now!" I said. I turned my head to see if my bottom looked abnormally large for my size.

"Come on," Hazel said. "Don't act like you don't know what's going on. We put the hairnets on, and now we want some answers." The three old ladies turned to each other and shrugged their shoulders.

I leaned over to Hazel. "I think they really

don't know what we're talking about." She didn't hear me. She was too busy begging the lunch ladies for more powers.

"Please, just tell me if I can trade in my banjo playing for a different power? Flying, or maybe laser vision, would be nice. Ooh, or how about stretching power? That would be awesome!" Her voice grew louder and louder. "Please!"

The lunch ladies looked more confused.

"Hazel, let's just get our lunch and go before we get in trouble," I suggested, but it was too late. Hazel was now in full-blown tantrum mode.

"I'm not leaving without answers!" she demanded, stomping her feet.

At that moment, a large hand rested on her shoulder. We looked up to see Principal Easton's big angry face staring down at us.

He called over to Ms. Flores. "I think this young lady will be eating lunch in the office today."

"But you don't understand," Hazel begged. "I need more powers!"

Mr. Easton didn't seem to care about Hazel's need for power. Hazel picked up her tray and followed him into the hall.

Scarlett and I took our food and sat down at the end of our class table. "Can you believe that?" I said. "They really can't remember anything about the superpowers. I guess we are on our own."

Scarlett bit into a carrot. "Great, it looks like I'm stuck with that hideous dress."

After lunch, we went outside and sat on the grass next to the soccer field.

"Hey, we get Izzy," Jackson yelled.

"We're not playing today," I called back.

Scarlett looked at Jackson and then back at me. "Hey, I think Jackson likes you," she said.

"Why would you say that?" I said. Scarlett knew as well as I did that all boys are disgusting. Although, for a disgusting boy, Jackson was kind of cute.

"Why else would he always ask you to be on his team, even before he asks Ben and his other friends?" Scarlett said.

I couldn't help smiling. "I don't know, maybe because I'm good."

"Hey, are you blushing?"

"No, I'm not blushing. I never blush. Why would I be blushing?" I covered my cheeks with my hands, suddenly feeling extremely nervous.

"I don't know, you just looked like you were blushing. No need to freak out."

"I'm not freaking out! And for the record, I wasn't blushing." I could feel Scarlett staring at me while I pulled up a few blades of grass and fidgeted with them.

"Hmm," Scarlett said. "I think maybe you are blushing, and maybe you actually like Jackson back."

"What do you mean?" I asked, feeling my cheeks again. "Why would you say that?"

"So, you don't deny it? Wow, Izzy, I can't believe this. You like Jackson!"

I stuck my hand over her mouth. "*Shhh.* I never said that. Plus, this goes against the whole 'boys are disgusting and stinky' thing that we all know is true."

"You like Jackson. Yep, I can tell. You can deny all you want, but—"

"Okay, maybe just a little. But promise me you won't tell anyone!"

"I promise," Scarlett said. Before we knew it, the bell rang, ending recess and our discussion about Jackson.

Chapter 6

The Villain Among Us!

Hazel was already sitting at her desk when we got back from recess. She immediately ran up and met us at the door.

"We have to talk," she said. Her eyebrows were low and serious, which was very unlike her. I'd only seen that face one other time in my life. It was at her birthday party last year when Ashley Campbell had just eaten Hazel's piece of birthday cake by accident; the piece with the huge frosting flower. I wondered why

Hazel looked so serious now.

Ms. Flores leaned over to Hazel. "Is there a problem?" Hazel quickly shook her head and returned to her seat. Something strange was going on. Ms. Flores kept her eye on Hazel all the way to her desk. Then she glanced over at Scarlett and me. We hurried and sat down.

The rest of the day lasted forever. Three people gave their career presentations. Brynn went last.

"My dad is a dentist," she said. "When I grow up, I'm going to be a dentist, too."

Brynn talked about the different things dentists do. "And if you don't brush your teeth every day, your teeth could look like..." She paused to create some suspense. "Like this!" She held up a large photo of someone's mouth with disgusting, rotten teeth. Some teeth were missing, and others were all greenish-black. We all gasped at the gross photo.

"Those look like your teeth, Hazel," Ben whispered, poking Hazel with his pencil. Hazel didn't even flinch. She just sat there staring straight ahead. Something was definitely wrong. Ms. Flores was also acting strange. Usually, she jokes around with the class, but that afternoon she was all business. When the final bell rang, we hurried to the door.

"What's going on?" Scarlett asked.

"*Shhh!*" Hazel answered. She tilted her head and pointed with her eyes to the door. As I grabbed my backpack, I had this strange feeling someone was looking at me. I turned my head to see Ms. Flores standing in front of her desk staring at us with her arms folded. We hurried outside.

None of us said a word until we were far away from the school grounds. Scarlett looked as nervous as I did even though neither of us knew what was going on. Once we were up the road a little farther, Hazel let out a deep breath.

"Okay, I know what crime we have to solve," she started. "I'll tell you at the clubhouse."

We hurried to my house and ran behind the big tree and sat on the ground. It felt like we were real secret agents about to receive our assignment.

"Well, what is it?" I said. "And what was all that weird stuff going on at school with Ms. Flores?"

"Okay, are you guys ready for this?"

"Yes!"

"Remember yesterday when you asked how we could ever find the bank robber? Well..."

Hazel paused and looked around as if someone might be listening. She leaned in.

"Ms. Flores..." She paused and looked around again.

"What about Ms. Flores?" Scarlett asked.

"She's the bank robber!" As soon as she said it, she covered her mouth with both hands. Scarlett and I looked at each other. I don't know who smiled first, but someone did, and we both fell over laughing.

"I'm serious. Can't you see it in my face?" Hazel had on the Ashley-ate-my-cake look again.

"You are serious, aren't you?" I said. "You'd better explain."

"I don't even know where to begin."

"How about at the beginning," Scarlett suggested. "When you were arguing with the lunch ladies, you got busted by Mr. Easton. Start from there."

"Yeah, okay. So, there we are walking down

the hall. I'm staring down at my tray wondering what I was going to eat first. Then I noticed that in all the commotion they forgot to give me a roll. So, I look up at Mr. Easton and ask him if I can go back to get my roll. 'No,' he says, 'you'll be fine without a roll today.' Then I tell him that doesn't seem fair since I paid for an entire meal. So, he says—"

"Holy cow, Hazel!" I interrupted. "Is all of this really important or can we just get to the good stuff?"

"Of course it's important. Rolls are my favorite part of the meal! Especially when they don't serve potato chips. Although, when they serve both on the same day... well, that's just pure heaven." She clasped her hands and closed her eyes dreamily.

"You know," Scarlett said, "it's probably okay to miss the roll every now and then. They're loaded with calories. You'd be better off asking for an extra apple or more carrot sticks."

"Why would I want a carrot stick when I can have a roll?" Hazel asked. "I'm talking rolls, not calories—"

"Yeah, but they're the same thing. You see—"

I threw my hands into the air. "Can we forget the roll, the carrots, and the calories, and just get to the point?"

Scarlett nodded and pretended to zip her mouth with an invisible zipper. Hazel took a deep breath and started again.

"Okay, so by the time we get to the office, Mr. Easton is so tired of arguing about the roll that he tells me to sit down at the small table, you know the one in front of Mrs. Hatch, the secretary, and he goes back to get my roll. So, as

I'm sitting there eating my roll-less lunch, Ms. Flores walks in to use the copy machine. They chat a little, and then she picks up her copy and walks out the door."

"Well, as amazing as that story is," I said, "I really don't see how making a copy makes her a criminal."

"Was she printing money?" Scarlett asked.

"On a copy machine? No, of course not."

"Did she steal something from the office as she left?"

"No, she didn't steal anything from the office. Let me finish." Hazel leaned in closer.

"About ten seconds after she leaves, Mrs. Hatch gets up to use the copy machine and notices that Ms. Flores forgot the original paper she was copying. It was still under the cover. Without looking at it, she hands me the paper and asks me to run it down to her. I'm mad because I still don't have my roll, but I say, 'sure' in that voice that lets people know that I'm not happy about it."

"Oh, I know that voice," Scarlett said. "It's the same voice I used when you asked for my cookie yesterday at lunch and I said, 'Fine,' but I really meant, 'no.'"

"Yes, that voice!" Hazel said. "I love using that voice!"

"So do I!" Scarlett said. "Especially when—"

"Okay, okay, what happened next?" I said.

"Right, sorry. So, I took the paper from Mrs. Hatch. And since I'm a very nosy person, I looked at the paper."

"That's for sure. You are the nosiest person I know," Scarlett agreed. "Remember when we had that sleepover, and my diary was on the top shelf of my closet. As soon as I left the room, you—"

"Ah! Forget the diary and the sleepover," I said. My heart was pounding. I needed to know what was on that paper.

"Sorry," Scarlett said, zipping her lips again.

Hazel pretended to hold a piece of paper as she continued her story. "So, I held it up and noticed it had some kind of diagram on it. It was like a map of a building. As I looked closer, everything was labeled; things like offices, restrooms, windows, and some red lines that were labeled *alarm*. Then I saw a big area in the corner that said *vault*. It was circled. At the top of the paper was written *Washington County Bank* and right next to it someone had written this Friday's date. Just then, Ms. Flores rushed back through the office door and ripped the paper out of my hand. She looked extremely nervous and said, 'What are you doing with that?'

"I didn't know what to say. Luckily, Mrs. Hatch, who didn't know what was on the paper, smiled and said, 'You left that on the copy machine. I asked Hazel to run it down to you.' She looked at her, then at me. She gave me an Ashley-ate-my-cake look and then left."

"So, what did you do?" Scarlett said. "Did you tell Mrs. Hatch?"

"What I wanted to do was to put on my lunch lady hairnet and take care of business. I wanted to scrunch her into a little ball and then kick her down to the police station like a soccer ball. But I got distracted because just then Mr. Easton walked in with my roll, and I was so hungry I stuffed the whole thing into my mouth. I tried to say something to Mr. Easton, but my mouth was full, so he couldn't understand me. Then he and Mrs. Hatch went into his office and shut the door. They were still in there when the bell rang, so I came back to class."

"Before we start kicking our teacher around town, don't you think we should be sure that she's really a criminal? Maybe there's some sort of explanation for this?" I said. "Think about it—our teacher, a bank robber?"

"Izzy's right," Scarlett said. "Maybe she just

likes to know her way around her bank. Or maybe she has a night job as a bank security officer and has to work on Friday. She does look like she's in really good shape."

"Are you serious? Why would she be so nervous? Why would she rip the paper out of my hands? I think she's planning on breaking into the bank on Friday night."

"What do we do?" I asked.

Scarlett pulled a notebook and pencil from her backpack. "We investigate!"

"What are you talking about?" I said. "We can't get involved with something like this."

"Sure, we can," Hazel said. "We're superheroes! We are in charge of the entire world. Plus, it's all coming together. Remember yesterday? Doesn't it seem strange that we just get these powers a day after another bank is robbed, and then this whole thing with the bank map miraculously gets handed to me? We were destined to be superheroes!

And we were destined to solve this crime."

"Well, I guess we sort of are superheroes, but I still don't—"

"Okay, let's take a look at the facts," Scarlett said, cutting me off. "One, this is Ms. Flores's first year at our school. And she's always talking about the different places she's lived. That is just like a criminal—always on the run. Two, Ms. Flores has a map of the inside of a bank. And three, she looked really mad and nervous when she saw you with the map."

"But remember, maybe she works there, or something, at night," I reminded them. Scarlett wrote that down as well. "We could go down to the bank and ask if Ms. Flores is working tonight."

Hazel jumped up. "That will be perfect! We can go as old ladies. You know, as

The Banjo-Picking, Karate-Kicking, Crime-Fighting Grandmas."

"The what?" I asked.

"You know,

The Banjo-Picking, Karate-Kicking, Crime-Fighting Grandmas.

That's our new name; I worked on it last night when I should have been doing my homework."

"Isn't that a little long?" Scarlett said, trying to repeat under her breath. "I don't think I can remember something that long. How about something shorter and to the point? Something like, The Ninja Grandmas."

"No, it's perfect just the way I said it," Hazel said. "I can see us now, on the front page of the newspapers and all over the internet—a photo of Scarlett holding two criminals over her head, and Izzy jumping in the air giving another bad guy a karate chop. And I could be in front, playing our theme song on my banjo while also giving a karate kick. And above the picture it reads,

'THE BANJO-PICKING, KARATE-KICKING, CRIME-FIGHTING GRANDMAS

SAVE THE CITY AGAIN!'"

"Before we're in any picture, I seriously have to do something about my clothes," Scarlett said.

"Come on, Scarlett," Hazel said. "You look great."

"*I look great?* How can you say that? I would rather wear something from last year's clearance rack than this awful outfit! It's just so... wait, that gives me an idea. Maybe we can stop by the mall on our way to the bank and look at some new clothes. I have some birthday money I've been saving."

"Yay!" Hazel said. "Let's go."

"I'm not sure about this," I said. "Shouldn't we be more careful about who sees us? Have you already forgotten our bike incident?"

"That was back when we were amateurs— now we're pros!" Hazel said. She pulled her lunch hairnet out of her pocket.

I was a little nervous but finally agreed. There was something about Hazel's enthusiasm that gave me confidence. "All right, let me go in and tell my grandma that I'm leaving." I ran inside quickly and hurried back out.

"Now, before we put our hairnets on, let's say our name," Hazel said.

"What name?" Scarlett asked.

Hazel rolled her eyes. "You forgot already? Remember: Banjo-Picking, Karate—"

"Oh yeah, that karate-kicking thing," Scarlett said.

"Do we have to?" I asked. "We're kind of in a hurry."

"Yes, we have to. It will be great. We can pretend that it's what we have to say before we turn into ninja grannies. It will make us feel more like superheroes instead of strong old ladies with saggy arms and big bottoms who can run fast. And don't worry, I'll help if you forget the words."

Scarlett and I both sighed. "Fine."

Hazel clapped. "Perfect! I'll start."

She held out her lunch lady hairnet and in a loud voice announced, **"BANJO-PICKING..."** Then she motioned to me to continue the next part, whispering, "Karate-Kicking" in my ear. I held out my hairnet and said, **"KARATE-KICKING."** Scarlett had her hairnet out, ready for her part. **"CRIME-FIGHTING GRANDMAS!"** she shouted. Then we put our hairnets on and—**POOF**— were back to superheroes.

"See!" Hazel said. "Didn't that feel good? It felt so official!" Her saggy double chin bounced and jiggled as she talked.

"Okay, that was kind of fun," I admitted.

Hazel did a few warm-up jumping jacks and toe touches and was ready to go. "And before I forget, I had better warm up my banjo picking." She plucked a happy song. "You know, Steve Martin was right when he said that you can't play a sad song on the banjo."

"Who's Steve Martin?" I asked.

"I don't know, he's probably some kind of banjo master. You know, it's part of that random banjo stuff I suddenly have in my brain. And by the way, what do you think about this theme music?" She started playing a different song on her banjo.

Scarlett and I looked at each other. "Theme music?"

"Yeah. For instance, when we're running after a bad guy, I can play this." She played a fun, speedy tune on her banjo. "And when we're about to fight someone, I'll play *this*." She began playing something else. "And I call *this* our victory song..." She plucked a bright happy song. Then she turned to me. "And *this*," she said, playing a slow romantic song, "is what I'll play when you are holding hands with Jackson."

"Scarlett!" I yelled, almost swallowing my false teeth. "You promised not to tell!"

"Sorry, it kind of slipped out. Hazel made me tell her."

"No, I didn't. When you went inside, Scarlett said, 'Guess who Izzy likes.' She didn't even wait for me to guess. She just told me."

"Who else have you told?" I demanded.

"No one. I promise."

Hazel's not very good at keeping secrets, so I made her pinky promise that she wouldn't tell either. We hooked our wrinkly old pinkies together and made the pact.

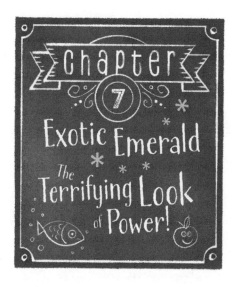

Chapter 7

Exotic Emerald

The Terrifying Look of Power!

"We have to hurry. My grandma said I have to be home in an hour."

"That shouldn't be a problem," Scarlett said. "With our superspeed, we can be there in no time."

Scarlett let Hazel ride on her shoulders this time, and we took off in a flash. Houses flew past like a blur while Hazel played our new theme music. Our saggy faces flapped around in the wind, and in no time, we arrived at the mall. We ran to the far end of the parking lot so no one would see two old ladies running around with a third granny riding on one of their shoulders.

"What kind of store are you looking for, Scarlett?" I asked.

"I usually shop at Somerset's. I'll just go to the grown-up section." We followed her down the center of the mall toward the large department store at the end.

I noticed heads turn as we passed by. "This is really embarrassing; everyone is staring at us."

"Of course they are. They've probably never seen superheroes before," Hazel replied. She gave people a wink and a thumbs-up.

"How would they know we're superheroes?" I said. "We just look old and weird."

"What? We don't look weird," Hazel said.

Scarlett stopped. "You've got to be kidding." She grabbed Hazel by the shoulders and turned her towards a large glass store window and pointed at her reflection. "Tell me what you see, Hazel."

Her hairnet was askew, her pantyhose were stretched tight over her chubby legs, and she had a banjo strapped to her back.

Hazel looked into the window. She put her hands on her hips and wiggled around a little. "I see one seriously beautiful superhero!"

Scarlett clapped herself on the forehead.

"I guess that's what I see, too," I said with a smile. "Only I see *three* seriously beautiful superheroes."

Scarlett gave in and put her arms around our shoulders. "You guys are right; we are beautiful, regardless of what we are wearing or what we look like. And you two are the best friends a girl—or a grandma—could ever hope for."

I looked at our reflection and hoped that in seventy years, when we actually were eighty years old, we would still be best friends.

We continued our walk to Somerset's department store, ignoring the stares. The women's department was just past the perfume and makeup counters. Scarlett went straight to a rack with pretty skirts and tops.

"May I help you, ma'am?" a nicely dressed lady asked.

"What?" Scarlett put her hand to her ear. The lady repeated her question, but this time much louder.

"MAY I HELP YOU?"

"Oh, yes, I'm looking for something like... like this," she answered, picking out a stylish skirt and holding it up to her.

"Is this for you?" the saleslady asked with a puzzled look.

"Yes, I think I'll try it on," Scarlett said. The lady led her to the dressing rooms along the back wall. Hazel was nowhere to be found.

I searched around all of the racks before hearing her voice. She was back at the makeup counter where the saleslady had offered to make up her face for free.

"Hey, Izzy, **free makeup!**"

I took a seat on a stool next to her. The girl behind the counter asked if I wanted to be next.

"No, thanks," I said politely. "We're kind of in a hurry."

The girl rubbed something into Hazel's face, telling her it would make her look ten years younger.

"That would make me less than one year old," Hazel laughed. The lady looked confused.

"Hey, can I have that color on my eyelids?" Hazel pointed to some bright green eyeshadow. She read the name out loud, "*Exotic Emerald*. Yeah, that one."

The lady explained all of the reasons why that color wouldn't be a good idea, but Hazel wouldn't listen.

"Pretty please, I really want that color."

The makeup lady gave in. (If there is anything more annoying than Hazel begging, it's Hazel begging as an old lady.)

"Oooh, and can I put on this lipstick, *Neon Passion*?" she asked, holding up the bright red lipstick tube. Again, the lady told her all about complementary colors and skin type, but Hazel wouldn't budge. She just begged more. Finally, the lady gave up and did everything Hazel wanted. Her eyelids were bright green, her lips were Neon Passion red, and the blush on her cheeks was a deep purple.

"Now this is what a superhero should look like!" Hazel announced. Catching herself, she added, "I mean, if there were any such things as superhero old ladies, this is exactly what they would look like."

The makeup lady politely excused herself, telling us she needed to help another customer, although no one else was around.

"Okay, ladies. Let's go," Scarlett said, walking up confidently in a brand-new outfit.

"Wow, you look great," Hazel said.

"Thank you." Then she saw Hazel's makeup. "Whoa, what happened to you? You look—"

"Beautiful? Fancy? Gorgeous?" Hazel suggested, making fashion model poses.

"Well, something like that."

We hurried out of the mall and ran to the bank a few blocks away.

"Maybe just one of us should go in," I suggested. "That way we won't make a scene."

"Good idea," Hazel agreed. "I'll go."

I looked at her in her new bright-green and red makeup. "I don't know. Maybe Scarlett should go. We don't want to scare them."

"What do you mean scare them? You think I'm scary?" She glared at me with those terrifying, bright-green shaded eyes and fluorescent-red lips.

A chill ran down my spine. "No, of course not. I just mean that maybe Scarlett should go because she, you know, has new clothes. So, she'll just look more official than you or me."

"Not me," Scarlett said. "I think you should go, Izzy. I'll get too nervous and mess things up."

"All right, I'll go."

Hazel and Scarlett agreed to wait outside out of sight.

"How do I look?" I asked.

"Bananas," Hazel said.

Scarlett agreed. She reached up and straightened my hairnet. "There you go."

"Thanks. Now how do I look?"

"Bananas," they both answered.

I took a deep breath and walked in. There were two people at the counter, and another waiting in line. A lady sitting at a desk stood up and asked if she could help me. She motioned to one of the chairs in front of her desk.

"Your friends are welcome to come in, too," she said.

"Oh, I'm here alone."

"So those aren't your friends at the door?" the lady asked. "With the hairnets, I thought maybe you work together."

I looked over and saw Hazel and Scarlett outside the door with their faces pressed up against the glass. *So much for staying out of sight*, I thought. "Oh, them. I forgot. You know how old people forget things," I said with a fake laugh. "They like the fresh air. They'll be fine."

"I was just stopping by to see if my daughter is working tonight," I continued. "I mean, my granddaughter. Yes, that's right, my granddaughter. She's a security guard here, or does something here after hours. Her name is..." I tried to remember if I had ever heard Ms. Flores's first name. "Her name is... well, she just likes to be called Ms. Flores."

The lady smiled. "The only security guard we have is Walter." She pointed to an older man standing by the door. "And there is no one else named Ms. Flores working here. Are you sure she doesn't work at another bank?" I could tell she thought I was confused.

"Oh, that's right," I said. "I think she works at a bank downtown. I'm sorry to bother you." I stood up and got out of there as quickly as I could.

Once outside, Hazel and Scarlett were all over me with questions.

"So, does she work here?"

"And did you get us some suckers?" Hazel asked. "You know they always have suckers at the bank."

I shook my head. "No."

"Do you mean *no, she doesn't work here*, or *no, I didn't get any suckers*?"

"No, she doesn't work here, and no suckers, either."

I was beginning to think Hazel was right about Ms. Flores. And if she was really going to rob the bank this Friday, we only had two days to do something about it.

Chapter 8
Time To Involve The Police!

Back at home, Grandpa was on the couch having a conversation with Jack about how to get Claire from math class to notice him. Jack sang his song to get Gramps' opinion. Gramps stopped him midway through the song.

"Listen, Jack," he said. "You know I love you like my own grandson, but—"

"I am your own grandson," Jack replied.

"Right. Which is why I feel it's my responsibility to tell you the truth. A girl doesn't want to hear someone she barely knows tell her that she is—how did you say it—the unsolvable algebra problem in his life, and without her you are drowning in an ocean of loneliness. That just sounds pathetic. And that part about planets crashing into the sun. What is she supposed to do with that, unless she is some kind of astrophysicist? And even then, it's probably—"

"It was *an ocean of desperation*, Grandpa. Do you want me to sing it again?"

"Good heavens, no, don't sing it again. What I'm saying is that girls like old-fashion romance." He leaned over and stared into Jack's eyes and raised his huge bushy eyebrows up and down as he talked. Gramps is bald but has enormous eyebrows that stick straight out from his head. It's as if when he went bald his hair decided just to grow in the form of eyebrows instead. "Girls want you to look into their eyes like this and—"

Jack scooted away from Grandpa. "Look, Gramps, I don't want to freak her out."

"Trust me. Once she's mesmerized by your eyes, ask her if she would like to study over at the malt shop."

"What's a malt shop?"

Just then Grandma called, "Dinner is ready." Gramps was up and in the kitchen in a flash.

My brothers and I held our breath as Grandma brought food to the table. Grandpa helped her. Fortunately, it was not liver. It was chicken in some kind of sauce that tasted awesome. Then she placed two Brussels sprouts on each of our plates. Those weren't so good. Gramps picked one up and popped it into his mouth.

"Ah, yes, if you want to grow up as strong as your grandpa," he said, "you'll want to eat lots of these."

Max rolled one around on his plate.

"They are to eat, not to play with, Maxwell," Grandma said.

Max picked one up and smelled it. "Can I get some ketchup?"

Max eats ketchup with everything. Especially with food he doesn't like.

As Grandpa finished his speech about the amazing power of Brussels sprouts, I decided to ask him and Grandma if they had ever heard of our superhero lunch ladies. I knew it was going to sound strange, but Grandma and

Grandpa had lived here forever; surely, they would have heard if there were news about old ladies doing something heroic over the years.

"Speaking of strong," I said. "This may sound weird, but have you guys ever heard of any older ladies around your age, or maybe a little older, who were superstrong and could run really fast, almost like they were, um, maybe old lady, ninja superheroes? Maybe you heard something in the news or sometime over the past few years. Or maybe they caught

criminals or something? I don't know, I'm just wondering."

Everyone put their forks down and stared at me as if I was speaking a different language. Jack took advantage of everyone's eyes on me to grab his Brussels sprouts and shove them into his pocket.

"No, I can't say that I have," Grandpa said, shaking his head. "Planets crashing into the sun, superhero old people—I must say, you kids have vivid imaginations."

That night, I could barely sleep.

The next day, we kept our eyes on Ms. Flores, trying to notice everything about her. Was she really a teacher, or was it all an act—all part of her plan? It made sense—become a trusted person in the community and then break into a bunch of banks and move on to the next town before anyone finds out. Plus, no one would suspect a teacher.

We sat on the grass at recess to have

a meeting.

"Okay, did either of you notice anything suspicious yet?" I asked.

Scarlett shook her head. "No, but did you see her shoes? Those would go so well with my black jeans."

"Well, I did see that she put her pencil behind her ear," Hazel said.

"She always does that," I said.

"Yeah, but this time she did it more like, I don't know, more like how a bank robber would do it. You know, with shifty eyes."

Just then, Jackson ran right through the middle of our meeting on his way to the soccer field. "Hey, Izzy, are you ready for the game tonight?" he asked.

A warm tingly feeling came over me. I wanted to say something clever, but the only thing that came out was, "Yeah." Jackson kept running.

"Hey, this would be a great time for that

romantic banjo song," Hazel said. She put her arm around Scarlett and pretended to be Jackson. *"Oh, Izzy, can I walk you home after the game tonight?"*

Scarlett answered back, in her best Izzy voice. *"Oh, Jackson, I thought you'd never ask."* Then they hugged and laughed.

"Knock it off, you guys! He'll hear you!" I looked up at Jackson to make sure he wasn't watching. Although, the truth was, I couldn't wait for our soccer games every week. I loved spending that hour on the field with Jackson.

"Okay, back to business," I said. "What

should we do about 'you know who'?" We only have tonight and tomorrow."

"Maybe we should go to the police and tell them about what you saw on that paper," Scarlett said.

I agreed. "Of course! We should have done that from the very beginning."

Hazel suggested that we talk to the police as old ladies. If for some reason Ms. Flores found out that we had told on her, she would not be happy. And if she truly was the thief that we thought she was, there was no telling what she might do to us.

That afternoon, we ran down to the police station. We recognized Officer Bagley right away. He stood up from behind a desk and leaned forward on his hands.

"Well, hello ladies." It was almost as if he was waiting for us.

"Hello, Officer Baggy," Scarlett said politely.

"It's Bagley, with an L," he answered. "How

is it that I've never seen you three before yesterday, and then suddenly in one day I get two calls complaining about older ladies disturbing the neighborhoods, specifically the neighborhood where I met you three yesterday? One was the bike-stealing incident. I'm still not exactly sure what happened there. And there was a second complaint from a frantic mother claiming that her children are terrified to play outside because they think old ladies with funny hats are falling from the sky." He looked us squarely in the eyes. "Is there something you three would like to tell me?"

We looked at each other and then back at him. Hazel finally spoke up.

"Listen, Baggy. Have you ever seen old ladies pick up cars or fall from the sky? We're just your ordinary citizens trying to keep our city safe. Sure, we may look strange. We may like to wear lunch lady hairnets and sneakers, and sure, my friend's bottom is not in proportion to the rest of her body. But if that's a crime then feel free to arrest us, because—"

"Ooh, don't arrest me," Scarlett interrupted. "I just got this new outfit yesterday. I would hate to have to trade it in for those orange jail clothes. Orange has never been my color."

Officer Bagley looked more confused than ever. He plopped back down in his chair. "Let's just start over," he said. "What can I do for you ladies?"

I stepped up to the desk. "Well, officer, we just came to let you know about a bank robbery that is going to happen in the future, Friday to be exact."

"Why me," Bagley muttered. "Okay, why don't you three have a seat." We sat down while he pulled a blank report from the desk drawer.

"Let's start with your names." He clicked the end of his pen.

"If it's alright, we'd rather not give our names," I said.

"Okay, no names." He ran his hand through his thinning reddish-blond hair, leaving it sticking up in spots. "Well, how about we begin with where you heard this information."

"I heard it when I was sent to the principal's office," Hazel said.

Officer Bagley looked up, raising one eyebrow higher than the other. "When you were sent to the principal's office?"

Scarlett and I tried to get Hazel's attention, but it was no use.

"Yes, I even had to miss recess. Anyway, I was waiting for the principal to bring me a roll from the lunchroom when our teacher walked in."

"Your teacher? Out of curiosity, what grade do you think you are in?" he asked. His face was turning red, and a vein was starting to swell on his forehead.

"Fifth grade, sir."

"What she means—" I interrupted, but it was too late. Officer Bagley dropped his pen and slid the blank report back into the drawer.

"That's it. You three really think you're funny, don't you?" he stammered. "Out of respect for the elderly, I am simply going to politely ask you to leave."

"But we're serious—you have to listen to us—because Friday night—"

"Goodbye, ladies." He opened the door and escorted us out. "And try not to pick up any cars or scare any little kids. I would hate to have to arrest three senior citizens for disturbing the peace. Good day." He disappeared back into the station.

"Wow, can you believe that?" Hazel said. "He didn't even care."

"Did you forget what we look like? Maybe an eighty-year-old lady being sent to the principal's office might have sounded just a tiny bit odd," I said.

"Sorry, I wasn't thinking," Hazel said sheepishly.

We thought about taking our hairnets off and going back in as our real ten-year-old selves, but we were too nervous that Officer Bagley would call our parents—or our school—and Ms. Flores would find out.

"We'll just have to take matters into our own hands," Hazel said. "I'm not scared of some fake-teacher-bank-robber, at least not when I'm an eighty-year-old banjo ninja." She made some karate chops and a kick in the air.

About halfway home we took our hairnets off on a quiet street behind a parked car. It was at that moment that I had a slight malfunction. My arms, face, and clothes all returned to normal. However, my backside didn't change!

"Oh my gosh! My bottom is still huge!" I yelled.

"Ooh, weird," Scarlett said. "How did that happen?"

"I don't know, I just took my hairnet off like always." I jumped up and down, trying to fix it. "What am I going to do? I have a soccer game tonight."

"What are you going to tell your parents?" Hazel asked.

"I don't know. My mom and dad are still away. My grandparents are staying with us."

Hazel suggested I tell everyone that a bee stung me. "Once I got stung by a bee and my thumb swelled up."

"As big as this?" I asked, pointing to my backside.

"Of course not. That's enormous."

Somehow that didn't make me feel any better. "Well, maybe my grandparents won't notice."

"How could they not notice?" Scarlett said.

That didn't make me feel any better, either.

We made it to Scarlett's and then went our separate ways. When I walked through the door, my grandma freaked out and wanted to take me to the doctor. I told her I accidentally sat on a bee and that the swelling would go away soon. "This happens all the time," I said.

"You must have sat on a whole hive," Grandpa joked.

Jack wasn't even fazed by it. "Hey, Iz, would you like me to write a song about that? I could call it 'Bees and Butts.' What do you think?" He sat down at the table and started humming to himself and making up some lyrics.

I was the tallest person when we sat at the dinner table. It was like I was sitting on a giant balloon. Max was laughing and poking me, thinking I had stuffed a pillow in my pants. Finally, I told him that I'd sit on him if he didn't stop.

I was humiliated and didn't want to go to the soccer game at all. But I knew we were going to be short a couple players tonight. A kid named Anthony had broken his leg two weeks before and was in a cast. And Jacob, our goalie, had just gotten his tonsils out. I usually wanted to do things to make Jackson notice me, but not like this. I grabbed my soccer ball—which I always bring with me to warm up—and we climbed into the car and drove to school. Grandma brought a blanket to sit on with Max during the game.

"Whoa!" Coach exclaimed. "Are you okay? Just tell me you can play."

There were gasps from the parents, and every kid on my team was laughing at me, including Jackson. Staying home and forcing our team to forfeit was sounding better and better.

"I'm fine. Just a bee sting," I said, taking my place on the field. It was a little awkward running, but I did okay. And I even blocked a kick with my bottom that saved a goal. So, I guess it worked out okay. Luckily, sometime during the first half, my rear end shrunk back down to normal. Grandma was relieved. So was I.

We ended up winning the game one to zero. As we walked to the parking lot, I noticed that Ms. Flores's car was still at school. I knew it was hers because my mom and I once saw her at the store loading up groceries.

Why would she be here so late? I wondered. It was starting to get dark outside, and from the parking lot, I could see that the lights in our classroom were off. The only lights still on were in Mrs. Peterson's classroom. I decided to investigate. I dropped my soccer ball and pretended to accidentally kick it over by

the school.

"Oops—I'll be right back, Grandma." I ran and picked up the ball. Then I snuck over to Mrs. Peterson's classroom window and peeked in. *What was she doing?* Ms. Flores was going through Mrs. Peterson's desk. Just then my grandpa honked the horn for me. Ms. Flores looked up. I ducked down and snuck back to the car.

Chapter 9

We Found it!

Scarlett and Hazel couldn't believe it when I told them about Ms. Flores the next day on the way to school. "Do you think she's stealing from Mrs. Peterson, too?" Hazel asked. Mrs. Peterson had been Scarlett's teacher last year.

"I wouldn't be surprised," Scarlett said. "Mrs. Peterson always wears nice things, and she has some pretty jewelry. She has a beautiful sapphire ring that she told us her grandmother gave her when she graduated from college. But she would never keep stuff like that in her desk drawer."

"We need to think about this," Hazel said. "Maybe she was just borrowing something, like a ruler or some markers. Or maybe she was looking for a sandwich." Hazel acted like a sandwich would be a normal thing to be looking for late at night inside a teacher's desk.

"No, she was digging through the drawer looking at different papers and looking through files."

"I think we need to find out more about Ms. Flores," Scarlett said. "But how?"

"Maybe we should sneak a peek into Ms. Flores's desk," Hazel said. "Maybe we'll find some clues."

We concocted a plan. Since my mom and dad were still out of town, my grandma was going to come to my parent-teacher conference tonight. I decided to tell her that they were canceled. Instead, Hazel would put her hairnet on and come as my grandma.

"This will be great," Hazel said. "I'll ask Ms. Flores about her background and where she used to teach. You know, find out more about her to see if she gets all squirmy. Then I'll ask her to take me to the office, or somewhere. While I'm distracting her, you and Scarlett search through her desk for clues."

At school, we tried our best to act normal. We didn't want Ms. Flores to suspect anything. Scarlett and Hazel's parent-teacher conferences were earlier than mine. They asked their parents if they could study together until eight o'clock at my house.

Everything was going perfectly. Grandma was relieved that she didn't have to go to parent-teacher conferences and told me I could go study with my friends after dinner.

We all met on the corner of my street. When the coast was clear, Hazel put on her hairnet.

"Whoa," I said. "You look even older than yesterday."

"Hey, is that any way to speak to your grandmother?" Hazel answered. We all laughed and headed down the road to school.

"So what time is your appointment?" Scarlett asked.

"I think six forty-five. We can check the schedule in the hall."

Hazel spent the rest of the way practicing being my grandma. She said things like, "My, how you have grown," and "You're just as cute as a button." Then she pinched my cheek.

Once at school, we walked to our classroom. There was one parent in the classroom talking to Ms. Flores and a man in the hall looking at the schedule. His face was about six inches from the paper.

"Excuse me," Hazel said, tapping the man on the shoulder. "May I have a quick peeksie at the list? I think I'm up next, but I'm not sure."

The man didn't budge an inch. "Wait your turn."

Hazel clenched her fists and lowered her brow. She was not going to stand for a man being rude to an old lady.

"How long does it take to read one name?" Hazel asked, leaning her shoulder into the man. "Excuse me," she said politely, knocking the man away from the list. He almost fell over. She quickly found my name. "Six-forty-five, right on time." She walked through the doorway, passing another mother who was just leaving. She turned and gave Scarlett and me a wink. We waited in the hall and listened. She always speaks loudly, so it was easy to hear.

"Hello, I'm Izzy's grandmother. Her parents are out of town this week, so I'll be filling in." She went a little overboard trying to be convincing. "Yes, that's exactly who I am. Just her old, wrinkly, slightly overweight grandmother. Yep, not her friend, just her grandmother. Well, I guess I'm also her friend, you know, as far as grandmothers go. But grandmothering always comes first. And I hope you don't mind me bringing the ol' General along with me," she said, patting her banjo. "I've got a gig tonight after this."

There was a long pause. I could only imagine what was going through Ms. Flores's mind.

"Could she just hurry up?" I whispered to Scarlett. "We only have fifteen minutes before the next parent comes."

Ms. Flores proceeded to tell Hazel all about what we were doing in class and what a good student I was. I wished my real grandmother were there to hear.

"While this is all very nice," Hazel interrupted, "I would like to have a quick tour of the facilities—the office, the lunchroom, perhaps the playground."

Ms. Flores explained that she had another parent coming in ten minutes and that the purpose of the meeting was to update her on my progress in the classroom.

"Well, the way I see it, young lady, part of a healthy school experience is the lunchroom facilities, the playground, and the administration offices. Exercise is part of a healthy education. And this hairnet I'm wearing represents fifty years of service in a lunchroom. I was a lunch lady when you were still in diapers. Also, I need to know that the office is not some kind of dungeon where kids are locked up."

"I can assure you that our office is perfectly appropriate for administering to our students' needs and—"

"Hold on right there, Missy," Hazel blurted out. "If you're unwilling to show me, it makes me wonder."

"Missy?" I whispered. We covered our mouths and giggled.

Finally, Ms. Flores gave in. "Okay, ma'am. We can poke our heads into the office and lunchroom, but I do need to be back here in a few minutes to meet the next parents." Scarlett and I hid around the corner. Once they passed us, we quickly ran into the classroom.

"Maybe you should wait outside the door and let me know if you see them coming," I told Scarlett as I rummaged through the desk.

There really wasn't much there—today's

math papers, waiting to be graded; the attendance notebook. I opened the small closet back by the cupboards, the one that was just for the teacher. Ms. Flores's jacket was hanging from a hook and her purse was on the shelf. There was nothing in the jacket so I quickly grabbed the purse, knowing that she and Hazel would be back at any moment.

"Oh my gosh!" I said out loud. Scarlett ran in.

"What is it?"

I carefully pulled the purse open wide and tipped it toward Scarlett.

Scarlett looked in and gasped. "A leopard skin mask?"

"What are the odds that Ms. Flores has a diagram of the bank *and* the same mask as the Feline Felon?"

Just then, we heard Hazel's voice. "Well, thank you for the tour. It looks like you have things under control here."

I closed the purse and quickly put it back in the closet.

"What should we do?" Scarlett asked frantically. We both looked around. "Hurry, to our desks, act natural." We slid into our chairs just as Hazel and Ms. Flores walked in.

"What are you two doing here?" our teacher asked. She glanced around the room, back to the closet, then back at us. Scarlett was shaking so hard her three bracelets were making a clanging noise.

I took a deep breath. "We were outside waiting for my grandma. We just came in to see if she was finished. When no one was here we just thought we'd wait at our desks."

"I see," Ms. Flores said.

"Well, thank you for the tour," Hazel said. "I've got to run. It's getting past my bedtime. Got to get that beauty sleep."

"I thought you had a banjo performance tonight," Ms. Flores asked suspiciously.

I grabbed Hazel's hand and pulled her away. "Grandma, let's go," I said. I mouthed "Sorry" to Ms. Flores, hoping she would just think my grandma was a little confused. Scarlett followed as we hurried out the door. Once we turned the corner, we ran into the bathroom. Hazel took her hairnet off.

"What's wrong with you two?" she said. "You look like you've seen a ghost."

I quickly looked in all four stalls to make sure we were alone. Scarlett and I explained the whole thing in about ten seconds.

Now Hazel was shaking, too. "What do we do?"

"I think we should go back to the police,"

I said. They both agreed. Just as we walked out, we bumped into Mr. Murphy and Mrs. Peterson.

"Excuse me," Mrs. Peterson said. She must have noticed the looks of fear on our faces. "Are you girls okay?"

We just stood there. I didn't know what to say. We'd just found out that our teacher was a bank robber and we were completely freaked out.

"Maybe we should tell," I told Scarlett and Hazel quietly in a shaky voice. They both agreed, knowing that we were in way over our heads.

"We really need to talk to somebody about something important."

"How about I take these girls down to my room and find out what's going on? I just finished my last conference," Mrs. Peterson said.

"I'll be in my classroom if you need me,"

Mr. Murphy said. "I've got one more parent who is probably already waiting for me."

"Okay, we were going to go to the police with this, but—" I started.

"Police?" Mrs. Peterson asked, sounding alarmed. She hurried us down to her class. We got to her room and took a seat around the table in the back of the classroom.

We told her everything, from the beginning (minus all that stuff about our new superpowers). She was especially interested when we told her that Ms. Flores was going through her desk the night before, and about the mask we found. We told her we were scared about telling on Ms. Flores in case she found out. When we finished, Mrs. Peterson just sat there. She looked as scared as we did.

"We tried to tell the police, but they wouldn't listen," I said.

"Have you told anyone else about this? Your parents, another teacher, anyone?" she asked.

"No," I replied. "We weren't really sure about Ms. Flores until tonight."

"I'm sure it's just a strange coincidence, but you are right; we should let the police take it from here." Mrs. Peterson rubbed her chin and thought for a moment. "This is what I think we should do," she said. "Why don't you let me take care of this. I'll go to the police right now, tell them everything you've told me. That way, even if Ms. Flores finds out, you three won't be involved at all. Leave it to me, girls."

I felt a huge sense of relief. Judging from the smile on Scarlett's and Hazel's faces, they felt the same. Mrs. Peterson gave us each a hug, and we left. We felt good knowing that we'd probably just saved a bank from being robbed and that Ms. Flores would be going to jail any minute.

As we walked down the sidewalk, Scarlett said, "Maybe we're not ready for solving crimes this big." Even Hazel agreed.

"Yeah. I really want to karate chop some criminals," she said, karate kicking the air at an invisible bad guy, "but maybe we should start out with smaller crimes, like guys cheating on tests or bullies picking on little kids. I can see it now: Ninja Grandmas rushing in on the scene, picking up a bully and scrunching him up and rolling him straight down the hall to the principal's office like a bowling ball. We can call it 'Bowling for Bullies.'"

Chapter 10

The Weirdest Music Video Ever!

I got home and was so nervous about what was happening with the police and Ms. Flores that I couldn't even focus. Luckily there was so much going on at my house that I was able to forget about it, at least for a while.

I walked in the front door to an unbelievable concert of Gramps, Jack, and Max. Apparently, after hearing the song Jack had written for math girl, Gramps had gone home to get his accordion to show him how to really write a love song.

"Iz, you're just in time," Jack said. "Can you video this masterpiece?"

"Um, sure. What are you guys doing?"

"Turns out Gramps is amazing on that thing," Jack said, pointing to the accordion hanging around Grandpa's neck. Plus, it gives my song to Claire an old-fashioned feel that balances out my ultra-awesome modern sound."

I'm not sure I would call Jack's playing ultra-awesome, but oh well.

Grandpa played a quick little tune. "Yep, I was pretty good back in the day. You're looking at the winner of the Wilson High School talent show's honorable mention award. And believe me, they didn't give that award to just anyone."

"Awesome," Jack said. "We will have to put that in the credits on the video: *Featuring award-winning accordionist Arthur Hernandez, AKA Gramps.*"

Jack handed me his phone for the video. "We are going to go through this one more time and then we will record it. Iz, you're kind of like a girl; will you listen to this as if you were Claire and tell me what you think?"

"*Kind of like a girl*?" I asked.

"You know what I mean."

"Not really, but whatever."

"Okay, here we go. Gramps, do you want to start us off with your intro solo? And Max, remember, you stand in the back holding up this drawing of a heart."

Gramps played something on the accordion. A few moments later, Jack started strumming. It didn't really sound like they were playing the same song, but they both seemed happy.

Midway through the song, Grandma came in and announced that it was time for Max to get his pajamas on.

"Can he wait until we do the video?" Jack asked. "I need the Maxman for the cute factor."

"I promised your mother that I would get Max to bed on time," Grandma said, pointing to her watch.

"Just one video, Janice," Gramps said. "And Max can go to bed."

"Grandma's name is Janice?" Max said, laughing.

While Gramps and Jack negotiated with Grandma, I went to the kitchen for a glass of milk and a snack. By the time I returned, not only had Grandma given in, but she was now singing backup. This was getting weird.

"Okay, Iz, we're ready," Jack said. "And Grandma, I loved that 'Ooooh yeah' part you did when I sing about the planets crashing into the sun."

Grandma gave him a thumbs-up.

I started recording the video on Jack's phone. Jack counted down, and Gramps started as before. Grandma swayed in the background. I zoomed out to get everyone in the video and

zoomed in on Jack when he was singing. Suddenly, walking around in a lunch lady hairnet didn't seem all that strange compared to what was going on in my living room.

"That was great!" Jack said after we finished. "Claire is going to love this!"

Grandma took Max to get ready for bed; Gramps stayed to help Jack write the perfect text to Claire before sending her the video. I went to my room.

Again, I didn't sleep very well. I just kept wondering what was happening with Ms. Flores. Did they find the mask? Was she in jail? What if they weren't able to arrest her? What if she remembered Scarlett and me being in the classroom alone when she wasn't there? And what if she saw me looking at her through the window when she was snooping around in Mrs. Peterson's desk?

It turned out that Scarlett and Hazel were wondering the same things. On our way to school Friday morning, Hazel asked, "Do you think the police believed Mrs. Peterson?"

"I hope so," Scarlett answered. "I was thinking about it all night."

Luckily, when we got to school our fears went away. The final bell rang, and there was no Ms. Flores. This was a good sign. However, when no substitute showed up ten minutes later, I began to worry. Surely, the police would have called the school to notify them of what had happened.

"I'll go to the office and find out what's going on," I announced. Everyone booed.

"Why would you do that?" Ben said. "Let's just sit here and relax."

"I'll be the teacher," Jackson said. He walked up to the front of the room, trying to walk like Ms. Flores and imitating her voice.

"Everyone, take out a piece of paper," he said. "I'm going to give you your spelling words."

The class laughed.

"The first word is *stinky*," he began. "Ben is very stinky. Everyone, write it down." He continued down his made-up list, reciting words such as *belch, puke, booger,* and other disgusting words, and using them in sentences. Our class was laughing so loudly that Mr. Burton from next door came over to find out what was going on. As soon as he discovered we didn't have a teacher, he called the office. In no time at all, Mr. Easton was in our class.

"I'm sorry, boys and girls," he said. "We

didn't receive a call from Ms. Flores this morning. Perhaps she's just late. We're trying to contact her now, and if needed, we will get a substitute for you shortly."

Mr. Easton stayed and read to us. After that, he tried to explain our math assignment. He stayed until it was time for lunch. Scarlett, Hazel, and I took our places at the back of the line as we walked to the lunchroom. On our way, Mrs. Hatch stopped Mr. Easton and told him there was a parent in the office who needed to speak with him.

"Why wouldn't the police tell the school about Ms. Flores?" Scarlett whispered. I could tell she was nervous by the way she was playing with the ends of her hair.

"I don't know. Maybe we should ask Mrs. Peterson about it," Hazel said.

"Better yet," I said, "what if we take a little field trip to the police station during lunch? Did you girls bring your hairnets?"

"I never leave home without it," Hazel said, patting her pocket.

Scarlett nodded and pointed to her small purse.

"Let's go," I whispered.

"Now? Before we eat?" Hazel complained. "I don't think that's such a good idea."

"Yes, now," I answered. "We only have forty minutes for lunch and recess."

"But I can eat fast," Hazel pleaded.

"Okay, just stay," Scarlett said. "We can handle this without you."

"What? Without me?" Hazel looked at us, then at the kids in the lunchroom who were already eating, then back at us. "Oh, all right, I'll go!"

Chapter 11

Captured!

We snuck away like we were going to the restroom. Once in the restroom, we put on our hairnets. We quietly slipped out the doors. With no one around, we ran like the wind all the way to the police station.

"Okay," I said. "We're just going to ask about Ms. Flores. We need to find out if they caught her last night. And why don't you just let me do the talking this time?"

They both agreed.

Scarlett held the door open, and we all walked in. "Oh no, not him again," I said. Officer Bagley had a paper plate on his desk with a donut on it and half a turkey sandwich. Papers were all over the place.

"Hello, Officer Baggy," I said. "I mean, Bagley. Sorry about that."

"Well, if it isn't our oldest elementary school kids with bank-robbing teachers. Shouldn't you be in class right now?" he joked.

"No, we're at lunch recess," Hazel blurted out. I looked at her and shook my head. She threw her old chubby hand over her mouth. **"Oops!"** she mumbled under her hand.

"Oh, I see," Officer Bagley said, smiling. "Just left the playground to come visit us? You know kids aren't allowed to leave the school without their parents."

"Look, Baggy, I would not have missed lunch if this weren't an emergency," Hazel said.

This was not starting off very well. I tried to explain. "The reason we're here is that we need to find out if our teacher was arrested. I mean, if my granddaughter's teacher was arrested."

Bagley wasn't taking us seriously. While we talked, he was putting some papers into files and doing other work. "Now, what makes you think this teacher was arrested?"

"Because she's going to rob a bank, and in her purse was—"

"Oh yes, the bank-robbing teacher," Bagley said, still fumbling with papers. "Why don't you simply talk to your principal? If there is a problem, your principal can call me." He smiled, thinking he was funny.

This was going nowhere. Scarlett, who had taken a small folding mirror and some lipstick from her purse and was applying it to her lips, spoke up.

"Okay, Officer Baggy," she began.

"For the last time, it's not Baggy, it's—"

Scarlett immediately held her hand up in front of his face, like she does to Hazel, stopping him from saying another word. "Listen, Baggy, do you see my friend here?" She pointed to Hazel, who was eyeing the donut. "She hasn't had lunch yet, and you don't want to see her when she is hungry and angry. So, I would suggest you listen to what we have to say, or I can't be held responsible for her actions."

"Excuse me, ma'am. Are you threatening a police officer?" Bagley asked, turning serious.

"Not at all," Scarlett answered. "I'm just

saying that—"

Just then, Officer Bagley noticed his donut was missing. Hazel had half of it in her mouth and was holding onto the other half, ready to finish the job.

"Hey, that's my donut." He reached for the other half, but Hazel quickly stuffed it into her mouth. I tried to calm everyone down before things got out of hand.

"Okay, Hazel, stop eating the nice police officer's lunch. Officer Bagley, if you can please just tell us what happened to Ms. Flores last night. We think she was arrested at Spring Valley Elementary sometime after seven o'clock."

"What are you talking about?" he said, raising his voice. Then he pulled the paper plate closer to him, guarding his sandwich from Hazel. "Listen, ladies, I hate to be harsh with you, but no one was arrested, no one has robbed a bank, and you three cannot continue to come in here and disrupt things. We are busy keeping the town safe. Please understand that. And you," he added, pointing to Hazel, "You stop eating other people's donuts."

"You shouldn't be eating donuts anyway," Hazel said. "I did you a favor. What if you need to run after a bad guy, but you're too out of shape to chase him, so he gets away?"

"Goodbye, ladies!" Officer Bagley sat down, picked up his pencil, and made some notes on a piece of paper. We turned and walked away.

We ran back to school with five minutes left of lunch recess.

"So, if the police didn't catch Ms. Flores, what is going on?" I asked.

"Maybe she got suspicious and ran," Scarlett suggested.

"We need to talk to Mrs. Peterson after school. Something isn't right."

The bell rang, and we hurried to class.

Our substitute never showed up, and Mr. Easton ended up teaching us all day. He mostly had us work on our own. Every half hour or so, he went to the office for a few minutes to take care of his official principal duties. When the final bell rang, we grabbed our backpacks and headed to Mrs. Peterson's class. We stayed outside her door until the last student left. As soon as she saw us, she motioned for us to come in.

"I'm so glad you're here," she said. "I need to talk to you three." We hurried in and sat down. She walked over and closed the door.

"What happened?" I asked. "Where's Ms. Flores? We asked at the police station, and they said no one has been arrested."

Mrs. Peterson's voice grew quieter. "You asked the police? What did they say?"

"They didn't say anything," Hazel said. "They thought we were making it all up."

"Okay, you three. I'm not supposed to tell you this, but..."

"But what?" we all said together.

"What I'm about to say cannot leave this room," she said. We all promised.

"This goes much higher than the police. What you have uncovered is so big that the FBI is involved. They have Ms. Flores in custody, and last night they uncovered more evidence after searching your classroom. They even set up a temporary lab to study the evidence right here at school in the basement. In fact, I know I promised that you wouldn't have to be involved, but I know they would love to speak with you about what happened yesterday."

We looked at each other and agreed.

I felt much better knowing that the FBI was involved.

"Great, follow me, girls, but don't say a word." Mrs. Peterson led us down to the end of the hall to the basement door.

"I've never seen anyone open this door," Scarlett whispered to me.

We stood there in the hall waiting for the last few kids to go home. Finally, when the coast was clear, she opened the door and guided us down the stairs. At the bottom were some desks and boxes that looked like they were fifty years old.

"So where are the FBI agents?" Hazel asked.

"Right here," Mrs. Peterson said. Suddenly, three men stepped out from behind a wall of boxes and grabbed us. They each put one hand over our mouths and held us tight with the other. A fourth man wrapped our wrists and ankles with a big roll of gray tape. He also taped our mouths shut.

"Nice work, boys. Lock them up in the back. We've got a busy night ahead of us!" Mrs. Peterson said. Then she bent down and stuck her face right into mine. "So sorry. I just couldn't have you three ruining my grand finale. It's nothing personal. I just like money. But don't worry, I won't leave you down here forever. I've written a letter to the police, letting them know where you are. They should get that letter in the mail in a day or two. By then, I will be long gone, out of the country on an island, grading math papers on the beach." She smiled and continued, "Well, maybe not grading math papers. So, until then, relax and enjoy. Ta-ta, girls."

The four men carried us to a storage room in the back of the basement and taped us to three chairs. They didn't tape Hazel's mouth very well and, somehow, she was able to get it off as they carried her.

"**Help!**" she screamed. "You'll never get

away with this, you fiend!"

"Fiend? Is that any way to speak with your fourth-grade teacher?"

Mrs. Peterson turned and calmly walked back to us. She personally stretched a new piece of tape over Hazel's mouth. "Oh, my dear little girls, I *will* get away with it—in fact, I already have. And by the way, thank you for tipping me off about Agent Flores. Thanks to you three, she won't be a problem, either. I found all sorts of goodies in her car, including her laptop computer. I used it to send a nice email from Agent Flores to her boss this morning, telling him that everything was a mistake and that there will not be any bank robberies tonight. So, the FBI will be at home enjoying their Friday night while I perform my biggest heist yet."

"Keep up the studying, girls." She turned and headed back up the stairs with the other bad guys.

Chapter 12

It's Grandma Time!

It was dusty and smelly in that basement room. Mrs. Peterson locked the door, but fortunately she left a light on somewhere. It wasn't too bright, but it shined through the cracks in the old door. We struggled to get free, but it was no use. After what seemed like forever, we were worn out. I wondered if Mrs. Peterson would really send the letter to the police, telling them about us. I didn't want to think about what would happen if she didn't.

As I was trying to think of some kind of strategy for getting out of there, Hazel started to wiggle again. And I'm not talking just a little wiggle. Her chair was bouncing around. She bounced so much she tipped over, landing with her head next to Scarlett's feet. She lay there, out of breath. We were doomed.

Feeling scared and discouraged, I couldn't think of any way out of this. As we sat there in the dark, Scarlett's eyes lit up. She wiggled one of her shoes off. I knew exactly what she was doing.

Ever since Scarlett was little, she could pick things up with her toes. It's amazing. Once, we were sitting on her couch doing homework when I accidentally dropped my pencil onto the floor. Before I had time to even bend over, she had reached over and picked it up with her toes just like they were fingers. Not only that, but she lifted her foot up and dropped the pencil back onto my book. Now, she was about to use that same skill to try to pull the tape off Hazel's mouth.

Hazel squirmed around at first, avoiding Scarlett's foot touching her face. But when Scarlett picked at the corner of the tape with her big toe, Hazel understood what she was doing. In no time at all, Scarlett ripped away the tape.

"Yeow! it feels like you tore my lips off!"

Hazel lay there and screamed for help, but it was no use. Everyone must have been gone by now. She wiggled closer to Scarlett's chair until she could reach the tape around Scarlett's ankles with her teeth. Hazel is as good at using her teeth as Scarlett is at using her toes. She gnawed through that tape like a rat through cheese. In a matter of seconds, Scarlett's legs and feet were free.

"I know!" Hazel cried. "Get my hairnet out of my pocket with your toes and put it on my head."

Still tied to a chair, Scarlett bent over and hobbled to where she could reach Hazel's pocket with her feet. Her toes wiggled around in Hazel's pocket.

Hazel laughed hysterically.

"That tickles!"

Scarlett rolled her eyes and kept trying. Finally, she was able to grasp the corner of the hairnet. From there, it was easy. With two toes, Scarlett simply grabbed it and pulled. And in another brief moment, she had it stretched out between her feet, and was placing it neatly on Hazel's head. **POOF!** Instant superhero!

"Yeehaw!" Hazel screamed as she broke through the tape on her hands and ankles. "Feels good!" She jumped around, karate kicking and punching the air. She quickly freed Scarlett and me.

Hazel took her hairnet back off. "Wait— we've got to say it first!"

"Say what?" I asked.

"You know." Hazel held out her hand.

"Banjo-Picking."

I added my hand on Hazel's.

"Karate-Kicking."
"Crime-Fighting Grandmas!"

Scarlett yelled. We all put on our hairnets. Hazel started playing our theme music while Scarlett put on some fresh lipstick. I karate kicked the door, smashing it wide open. We raced up the stairs and straight to my house. We pulled our hairnets off and ran inside.

Scarlett and Hazel called home to see if they could hang out at my house like always.

"I'm just mad!" Hazel said. "Forget about working on smaller crimes. I'm ready to get back to busting heads." We all were.

"No one ties me up, locks me in a basement, and gets away with it," I said.

Scarlett held up her pinky. "And no one makes me break a nail and gets away with it."

"So, what's the plan?" Hazel asked. She and Scarlett both looked at me as if I had the answer.

"First, we'd better call the police and let them know Mrs. Peterson is on her way to rob the Washington County Bank. She's probably already there." Scarlett handed me the phone and we called 911.

"Hello," I said. "This is an anonymous tip. The Washington County Bank is being robbed. Come quickly."

"Who is this?" the voice asked.

"That's not important. Just get someone there."

We flew down the stairs, out the door.

"Do you think they've already robbed it?" I asked as we ran behind the trees.

"There's only one way to find out," Hazel said. "Let's get down there." She ripped her hairnet out of her pocket and held it up for our superhero routine. Scarlett and I joined in.

"Banjo-Picking!"

"Karate-Kicking!"

"Crime-Fighting Grandmas!"

"Alright, girls—I mean ladies, or whatever we are—let's rock!" Hazel yelled. She sat on

Scarlett's shoulders and played our theme music as we raced down to the bank.

Everything appeared normal. People were walking in while others were leaving. A car was just entering the drive-through.

"Let's go check it out," I said. We cinched up our pantyhose and walked in. We scanned the whole place as everyone inside stared at my two friends and me.

"Looks fine," Scarlett said. "They must not have come yet." We went back outside.

"And here come the police," Scarlett said, using her supervision. They're about a half a mile down that road. "Quick, find someplace to hide. If it's Officer Baggy, he'll never believe us." We ran behind a minivan parked a few feet away.

Unfortunately, just as we crouched down, the engine started up, and the minivan drove away, leaving us huddled down in plain sight.

Now I could see the police cars, too. There

were four of them and they were just about to reach the parking lot. "Quick, up here," I yelled, pointing to a tree in front of the bank. I jumped up about twenty feet into the tree. Scarlett and Hazel climbed up as fast as they could.

We all sat on a thick branch high in the tree. "Be really quiet," I said. Fortunately, we made it up before they saw us, because leading the way was Officer Bagley himself. Four other officers stayed behind their cars while Bagley and three more cautiously made their way to the door. A lady walked out of the bank and held the door open for the policemen. They walked in and two minutes later were back outside. He and his partner walked over and leaned against the tree right under us.

"False alarm," I heard him say to someone on his radio. Then I heard a very scary sound— the sound of wood cracking. Before we could move, the branch broke, and we fell twenty feet, onto Officer Bagley and his partner.

"you three!" he said, struggling to get out from under Hazel. "Old ladies falling from the sky. This is all making sense now."

"Oh, hello Officer Baggy, sir. What are you doing down there?" Hazel asked.

We rolled off the officers.

"Listen, you three. You've just earned yourself a trip to the station. Telling stories about teachers and bank robbers is bad enough, but causing four cars and eight officers to leave their posts on a false alarm is not something we take lightly."

"We're really, really sorry, Officer Baggy," Scarlett said. "Please don't take us to the station."

"We promise, we'll never call again," I said.

"Plus, we're old," Hazel added. "We don't want to spend the last few precious days of our lives in jail."

We begged and begged, promising to be

good. Finally, his partner grabbed him by the arm. "Come on, let's move out."

Officer Bagley furiously brushed the leaves from his uniform. His face was bright red. "Okay, read my lips, ladies. **No more!** No more causing problems, no more stories, no more phone calls, nothing!" He stomped back to his car and yelled,

"Move it out. We're done here."

All four cars drove away.

"Now what?" Scarlett said. "Maybe Mrs. Peterson really isn't coming."

"No, she'll be here. Now that we know her secret, she needs to get the money and disappear."

Hazel started playing a sad song on the banjo.

"What are you doing?" we asked.

"Just setting the mood," Hazel answered. She swayed back and forth as she played.

Scarlett walked toward the bank door.

"Maybe we should wait inside."

Hazel stopped playing. "Yeah, I could use a sucker."

There were only a few people inside; about ten workers and five customers. The clock on the wall said five o'clock. "They only have an hour until the bank closes. The news said all of the other banks had been robbed while they were open. Maybe we should just wait."

"I'll go get some suckers," Hazel said.

She walked up to the teller and grabbed a few suckers from the glass bowl on the counter. We stood there eating them while the bank workers stared at us. Several walked by asking if we needed any help.

"Just waiting for a friend," I said.

Hazel crunched down on her sucker. She pulled the empty stick from her mouth. "I'll go get a few more of these."

"May I help you?" the bank teller asked as Hazel dug through the bowl.

"Yes, I think you are out of orange suckers. Are there any more?" The lady shook her head and apologized.

I have to admit, one of the benefits of being old was being able to do stuff like that. There is no way the bank would let kids stand around eating sucker after sucker without making them leave or calling their parents. But when you're an old granny, you can do whatever you want, and people just smile.

Hazel now had two suckers in her mouth and one in her hand. Then she turned to me. "Can you hold these?" She pulled the two suckers from her mouth and handed them to me.

"Gross! What do you want me to do with these?"

"I'm trying to mix different flavors together to see how they taste. I've already used these."

Just as I took the sucked-on suckers, a man yelled, **"Hands up!"** It scared me so bad I threw the suckers in the air. One landed in Scarlett's hair and the other shattered on the floor.

"Everyone down on the ground!" We all dropped to the floor. Eight ninjas in all black clothes and black ski masks were instantly all over the bank. Two jumped up on the counter by the sucker bowl and the other six were spread out, making sure nobody moved. Then, Mrs. Peterson walked in with her mask and a large flowery hat on.

"Thank you, boys," she said as she strolled past us and straight to the vault. She hummed as she began filling bags with money.

The men didn't pay much attention to us—

three harmless old ladies. I leaned over to Scarlett and Hazel. "We need to take these guys out. Mrs. Peterson is nothing without them."

"I'll make a scene and you guys sneak up on them," Hazel said.

"Okay, but how will we—" Before I could finish, Hazel was up.

"Hey, you guys in the black masks. How about a song?" Hazel began to play our fighting theme music while she danced around.

The men didn't know what to make of it. One of them put his hands up to his ears. **"Stop that!"** he cried. Hazel ran around and played even louder.

"Let's do this!" Scarlett yelled. She jumped up and in one leap tackled the bad guy with his hands over his ears. She picked him up over her head and threw him across the bank at one of the ninjas on the counter, knocking him off and sending the sucker bowl shattering on the floor.

Hazel's banjo playing was driving them nuts. It was like blowing one of those whistles that sends dogs howling.

"Keep playing, Hazel!" I said, before I ran straight after one of the others who had his eyes shut and his hands pressed against his ears. I dove, ramming my head into his stomach, launching him through the air and crashing against the wall.

When Hazel wasn't looking, a ninja jumped and kicked her banjo from her, sending it across the room.

"No one messes with my banjo!" she yelled.

The ninja tried to kick her, but Hazel caught his foot and with one hand swung him around by his leg like a rodeo cowboy with a lasso before sending him flying over the counter.

As a different ninja bent over to grab the banjo, Scarlett took out her Laser Lips and

laser beamed him in the backside, sending him to the floor screaming.

Another masked robber pulled the fire extinguisher from the wall and hurled it at me. I turned just in time, and it hit my gargantuan bottom. The fire extinguisher bounced off and hit the bad guy squarely in the nose, knocking him unconscious.

Scarlett was exchanging karate chops and kicks with a ninja by the front door. As she blocked his kick with her hand, she realized that she'd broken her fingernail. She immediately stopped and looked at her hand. "Seriously? You had to break my fingernail? That's the second one today!" He kept swinging and she easily dodged each attempt as she continued examining the damage to her fingernail."And I just painted these yesterday."

"Go find Mrs. Peterson!" I yelled.

"Got it!" Scarlett called back. She spun in the air sending the ninja flying with a superhero kick before heading to the vault.

"So, you want to play tough, do you?" Hazel yelled as two men closed in on her. "I call this one my *bad-guy-going-to-jail* song." She played even faster and louder. The bad guys couldn't take it. Both of them fell to the floor holding their ears, begging her to stop. "Hey, I think now I know why I have this banjo,"

Hazel yelled. "Bad guys can't stand it! It's awesome!"

Just then, one of the guys on the floor got up and lunged at her.

"Hazel! Behind you!" In a split second she spun around and whacked him with her banjo, sending him crashing into a desk.

"Wow! Did you see that? I think I know another reason I have this banjo!"

The last guy had stuffed tissues in his ears to drown out Hazel's powerful banjo. He pulled a set of nunchucks from behind his back and started swinging them every which way while running toward Hazel.

"Two can play at that game," she said. She blocked the whirling nunchucks. "Come on, is that all you've got?" she taunted, dancing around and blocking every swing. "Now watch this." She threw the spinning banjo high in the air like a baton twirling in a parade. As the bad guy looked up, Hazel jumped, and with a roundhouse karate kick, knocked him unconscious to the floor. Without looking up, she reached out and caught her banjo.

I was so entertained watching Hazel that I didn't notice two ninjas get up from the floor and dive at me from both sides. I quickly jumped ten feet in the air just as they dove at me, causing them to crash headfirst into each other. I landed on them with a double kick to make sure they wouldn't be getting back up.

"I am loving this banjo!" Hazel said, unwrapping two suckers and enjoying a victory treat.

Just then, one last ninja got up front the floor and ran toward Hazel.

"Look out!" I yelled.

She spun around and, without thinking, pulled the two suckers from her mouth and threw them at the ninja. They hit him squarely on his face.

Disgusted with Hazel's slobbery suckers,

he stopped to pull them off. I immediately jumped and karate chopped him to the floor.

Hazel high-fived me and then walked up to the floored criminal and stuck her round face in his. "That's right. No one messes with the Banjo-Picking, Karate-Kicking, Crime-Fighting Grandmas!" She strutted around him like a football player after taking down the quarterback.

As Hazel and I congratulated each other, Scarlett shouted from the vault.

"She's gone! Mrs. Peterson's gone! She must have slipped out the back."

We ran outside just in time to see a van screeching out of the parking lot.

Hazel jumped into my arms, "She's getting away! Throw me at her van!"

"Why don't we just run after her," I asked. "You can wait here for the police."

"Come on! Those guys are out cold. Plus, Walter, the security officer, has everything under control here," she begged. "He's on the phone with the police right now."

She was right, and we didn't have time to argue. I lifted her over my head and threw her as hard as I could toward the speeding van. Scarlett and I caught up right as she landed on the roof of the van.

"yeehaw!" Hazel howled. She began playing the chase theme music as she rode on the roof. The music was causing Mrs. Peterson to swerve all over the place.

"Stop that hideous noise!" Mrs. Peterson yelled. Scarlett and I ran up on both sides of the van. I knocked on her window and smiled. She looked astonished to see an old lady running alongside her car. She almost crashed when Scarlett knocked and smiled from the passenger side.

Hazel popped her head down in front of her windshield. "Hello, Mrs. Peterson! Nice day for a drive!"

Mrs. Peterson swerved out of control. Unable to see with Hazel's big head in her way, she crashed into a tree, sending Hazel flying into some bushes.

Without thinking, I tore the door right off of the van to see if Mrs. Peterson was all right. We noticed someone wiggling around in the back seat. Scarlett opened the side door to find Ms. Flores tied up. Other than a bump on her head from the crash, she was just fine.

"You ladies. Who are you? How did you..."

She rubbed her head, looking very confused.

"I think you hit your head pretty hard, Ms. Flores. Why don't you sit down and rest."

"How do you know my name?"

"Oh, that? Well, we, um..." As I tried to come up with an answer, Hazel walked up.

"Hello, Ms. Flores," she said.

"You're Izzy's grandmother."

A paramedic interrupted and they transferred Ms. Flores to an ambulance.

Four police cars showed up with lights flashing and sirens blaring. Officer Bagley was the first one out of his car.

"What took you so long, Baggy?" Hazel said. "Did you stop for donuts?" She reached over and patted his stomach.

He stood there speechless, rubbing his hands through his hair. "What happened here? How did you..." He looked at us, then at the van, then back at us. "I think I owe you three an apology."

We just smiled. "That's not necessary," I said.

"Yep, just doing our job," Scarlett added.

Hazel played our theme music one more time. "And don't forget," she said, "if you're ever in a bind, you know who to call." Then we all joined in:

"The Banjo-Picking,

Karate-Kicking,

Crime-Fighting Grandmas!"

We turned and headed down the street into the sunset. Well, not really into the sunset, but it seemed like that would have been a good ending.

On our way home we slipped behind some bushes and took our hairnets off. We couldn't stop talking about our first real adventure as superheroes. We laughed as we relived every karate chop, whack with the banjo, and ninja move, over and over. Yes, we had solved our first crime, and we all knew that there was no way it would be our last. We vowed at that moment to take down every bad guy in our town—maybe even in the world.

We walked home wondering if we would get the reward money and what we would spend it on. Scarlett was going to spend all of her share on new clothes. I just wanted a new bike. As for Hazel, she decided that she would buy the biggest, most expensive box of donuts ever, and maybe even send one to Officer Bagley.

The End

epilogue

Monday morning at school, everything seemed strangely normal. Ms. Flores was still our teacher. She started the day with the usual subjects as if nothing had happened. Ben was still bugging Hazel every chance he could. At noon, the old lunch ladies plopped corndogs onto our trays without even looking up. It was as if last week had never even happened. The only thing out of the ordinary was that Hazel was actually prepared for her career presentation. Since Ms. Flores was out last Friday, we hadn't finished them. Hazel was the last remaining student to present.

"And for my career, I tried to decide between a superhero and a professional banjo player." The class erupted in laughter. Ms. Flores surprisingly didn't say a word.

"But after thinking about it," Hazel continued, "I thought, *why should I have to choose between these two amazing jobs?*" She turned on some banjo music in the background while she discussed all the reasons the world needed superheroes and banjos. Still, Ms. Flores sat quietly.

Everyone loved the music and Hazel kept the class entertained with different ways a superhero could use a banjo. They were still asking her questions when the final bell rang.

We grabbed our backpacks and headed home to do our homework together. Once in my room, I opened my pack and noticed a large yellow envelope. "What's this?"

"I've got one too," Scarlett said.

Hazel pulled out a similar envelope.

Inside, they each contained a brief note:

Thank you for your help, girls. Your secret is safe with me.

We have much more work to do! This is just the beginning!

Amazing BANJO Pickin' Facts

TOP 10

1

When was the banjo invented?

Over 400 years ago. It was probably invented by the oldest known lunch lady.

2

Is the banjo the greatest instrument in the world?

Absolutely!!!

3

How many strings are on a banjo?

It depends on the type of banjo.
Usually either 4, 5, or 6 strings.

4

What instrument should be in every kind of band?

A banjo of course!

5

What should you do when you feel sad?

Play a banjo!

6

What should you do if you really want to bug your brother or sister?

Practice your banjo ALL DAY LONG!

7

Does Mike Knudson, the author of this book, play the banjo?

Yes!

8

Does Mike Knudson play the banjo well?

Not really, but he keeps playing anyway!

9

Does Mike Knudson drive his family crazy with his banjo playing?

Yes, regularly!

10

Does he care?

Nope.

Bonus Audience Question

Which is more annoying, a banjo or bagpipes?

Mike Knudson

Mike is an award-winning author who loves writing about

quirky friends whose lives never seem to go as planned.

He lives by the words of Charlie Chaplin,

"A day without laughter is a day wasted."

You can learn more about Mike at

www.mikeknudson.com

Vaughan Duck

Vaughan loves drawing pictures that make kids giggle.

He lives downunder in Australia where it's always sunny.

You can learn more about Vaughan at

www.vaughanduck.com

Made in the USA
Monee, IL
24 November 2023

47191331R00148